Gypsy Cradle

Andrea Drew

DEDICATION

For Maria Erai-Kingi, the best friend anyone could ever
ask for.
You know why.

CONTENTS

Gypsy Cradle

ACKNOWLEDGMENTS

Thanks to my editors Therese Arkenberg and Hazel Jia, for taking my ramblings and turning them into almost coherent. Thanks also to my beta readers for your valuable feedback early on.

1 PROLOGUE

Prologue

Monday 21ˢᵗ January, 9.36am

Christie leaned forward in her office chair, which creaked as she bent toward the monitor. The morning coffee tasted good, and she let it cool on her desk. Shuffling her chair closer to the screen, she grasped the mouse and clicked on the first email. Monday mornings were usually frantic and today was no exception.

Her stomach twisted, and she sat up as a wave of nausea hit. She lifted a hand to her temple, rubbing at the ache in her head.

What is wrong with me? I felt fine earlier.

As another wave of nausea hit, she knew something was wrong, very wrong.

Oh god, I can't vomit here, not at work.

She breathed slowly in an attempt to calm herself, and tentatively moved up from her seat, before sitting back down.

Bad idea. I don't think I'll make it to the bathroom. Oh god what do I do?

The lights seemed piercing, and she blinked. Prickles raced across her arms, which were cold and clammy. The thick warm suffocating air meant she struggled to catch her breath.

Her heart was hammering. It banged so loudly and fiercely that surely someone could hear it. John at the next cubicle was on the phone in an intense client discussion about a design project. Christie didn't understand any of it. She rarely suffered headaches or nausea.

"Jawwwwn," she groaned, trying to get help, but the word came out slow and slurred. Saliva dribbled from the corner of her mouth.

The room began to spin, slowly at first, then faster, until she was on a dizzying roundabout that culminated in her fall from the chair. She landed on the soft pile carpet with a thud.

John's head bobbed up over the top of his cubicle. His eyes widened. "Christie?" Christie had collapsed next to her desk, and he was up and out of his chair in an instant. "Oh my god, Christie!"

John squatted by her and, within a few seconds, Elle and Jason, two other designers, crowded around.

"Oh my god," breathed Elle.

"Call an ambulance!" screeched John, sending Elle and Jason scurrying, as he checked Christie's airway.

She was breathing, thank goodness, but unconscious. Another staff member appeared in the doorway and froze, coffee cups perched in midair.

"Don't crowd her," said John, putting one hand out. "If you want to help, make sure the bloody ambos know what to expect."

John stayed with her until the ambulance arrived. Once he'd briefed the paramedics, he turned to see shocked employees milling around, murmuring their concern. He followed the paramedics out to the ambulance as they loaded Christie in. He stood with arms crossed as it left.

He hoped she'd be okay. It didn't look good.

***

Friday 18th January, 9.30am

The day that I learned Christie's life was in danger started like any other. In fact, if anything, it was more pleasant than usual. Connor had the night off from his duties as senior detective at Carlton police station and I was looking forward to wine, dinner, song and possibly a roll in the hay if the stars aligned themselves correctly.

After a quick shower and breakfast, I headed to my study, coffee in hand, its delicious rich smell drifting upward. While my study was small, it was perfect for my needs. A beautifully varnished desk with a green antique writing lamp perched on the corner and the window before me allowed a view of my tiny but trim garden.

Today was one of those days when all was right with the world. After checking my emails and replying to two enquiries, I carefully retrieved a manila folder from the middle of a precarious pile. I'd just got into the writing zone, getting my mental teeth into a proposal for an electrical company, when I felt the buzz of my mobile phone. For a moment, I hung indecisive, wondering whether to abandon my train of thought to answer it. Then I saw that the caller was Leah, my younger sister.

"Leah," I answered curious, but in a tone much friendlier than it had been a year prior. We'd reached a new level of understanding and tolerance since Connor's nephew almost killed me, having learned how losing each other forever could feel.

"Gypsy, how goes it?"

I heard the slight wobble in her voice. "What's going on, Leah? Are you okay?"

"Yeah, I'm fine, really I am."

I called bullshit. Leah wouldn't ring me just to chew the fat with me; we didn't have that kind of relationship. Something was up, and given a couple of prods, I was confident she'd spill the beans.

"Pull the other one, love, it plays jingle bells. What's going on?" A bird bobbed on the front lawn as I waited for her reply. At first, all I got was a snuffly breath and some watery sniffing.

"Leah, don't leave me in mystery like this, what the hell is wrong?"

"It's that stupid bitch, Rita. She's resurfaced."

Great.

Around the time Connor's twisted nephew Aaron had kidnapped a police employee and left me for dead in an alleyway, Leah was going through a major upheaval in her marriage. She'd found Paul's phone one Saturday afternoon while he was having a nap, and was devastated to discover a pathetic sexting affair with a woman from work.

Of course, I hadn't realized at first that the other woman was Rita, a usually reasonable member of the book club. Not quite my cup of tea, but well-liked by Chloe and Matt. Rita, a friend of Chloe's, seemed personable and funny, and I'd warmed to her over time. However, after listening to Rita's brags about her sizzling fling with a married guy from work and learning the name of Paul's other woman, I'd been shocked. I put two and two together, which led to a parting of the ways between us. Leah of course alternated between fury, blame and inconsolable grief. Mainly fury.

Turning away from the window, I reached for my mouse and minimized the screen that was beeping quietly. Yet another email, probably spam. "What do you mean resurfaced? How? Did you find more messages on his phone?"

"She turned up here yesterday," said Leah, her voice cracking.

"Are you serious? What for?" Rita and I hadn't exactly been on the best of terms since her little electronic love tryst had been uncovered nearly a year ago. What was Rita thinking? The few times she had mentioned it to me we'd clashed, purely because she thought having an affair by mobile phone with a married man was hilarious, a bit of a giggle. Chloe and Matt, the two other members of the book club, had tried to talk me around but I'd never gone back. I'd maintained my friendship with Chloe, but the topic of Rita was off limits and had never been brought up again.

I had only been able to resume civilized relations with the woman in the last few months. I clenched one hand into a fist, wanting to let Rita have it.

"She came to see me yesterday. She must have been bloody stalking me. How else would she know I was home?"

Heat rose in my face.

"But why was she there? What did she say?" I said, incredulous.

"She said she was curious and wanted to meet me in person. The conversation lasted all of two seconds. I told her to never contact us again and slammed the door in her face."

Plus a few choice verbs, knowing how Leah unleashed her temper during fits of anger.

I wondered what sort of fresh hell the news had injected into their marriage. Paul had been dutifully contrite and remorseful, but it had taken four months of marriage counseling before their relationship was able to regain its equilibrium.

"I'll go and see her," I said, hearing the hard edge in my voice.

"No don't, please don't. I've already had it out with Paul and he says he knew nothing about it. For once, I believe him. He doesn't have the same phone number anymore. I don't think she'll show her face again."

"Want me to come over?"

"No, not now. We're having a casual barbecue here on Sunday. Come over then, it'd be nice to see you. Renee misses you."

I grinned and imagined a small smile creeping across Leah's face. She knew that using Renee for advantage would work with me, every time. "Okay, well, stay in touch. I'll see you Sunday. I'll bring something with me. Take care, hey?"

"Yeah, okay." The phone beeped as Leah hung up.

I pushed myself up from the office chair and dropped the phone to my desk with a clunk. As I paced the small room, I fought the urge to grab my keys and race over to see Rita. What was she thinking? I should give myself time to calm down, but damn it, someone needed to shake some sense into the woman.

CHAPTER 1

Friday 18ᵗʰ January, 6.07pm

Christie had told him about her grumpy but supportive boyfriend. Stories of Ryan cooking for her, caring for her, holding her as sobs racked her bony frame after the death of her grandfather. Ryan might have been abrupt at times, but supportive, no two ways about it. The little things he'd done to show he loved her had spoken volumes to both Christie and Brenton. Cooking small meals to tempt her into eating again, arms draped across her shoulders, tucking her into bed, washing her hair, bringing home books she loved in the hopes of distracting her.

Brenton stared at the computer screen, deep in thought. Ryan was the perfect guy. Good looking, trim, strong and determined, yet caring. Brenton raised his fingers to his collarbone, tracing its edges. He'd imagined him, dark, hot, stunning in every way. Brenton could almost taste the sweat on Ryan's chest, salty and acidic, imagining how it would feel to grasp a handful of the dark brown mane and slide a tongue down his chest.

Brenton wasn't stupid. He knew Ryan preferred women, that he'd been with Christie for almost a year and was as loyal and steadfast as a rock. It didn't stop him fantasizing about their life together, though. Walking hand in hand along the beach, hearing waves splash onto the sand, cooking together in his newly renovated white kitchen, the smells of garlic and basil surrounding them as they kissed and stared into each other's eyes.

Ryan was so damn *perfect*.

It had happened slowly, falling across him like a second skin until before he knew it; he was in love with a guy he'd never met. Maybe he should have stopped Christie from pouring out her heart and soul, grief consuming her as she described her grandfather's death and the way Ryan had been there for her.

Christie's grandfather Ray, her mother's father, had died four months ago, and Brenton knew the grief had practically burned her alive. She'd taken a week off and arrived back in the office with eyes red-rimmed and shoulders rounded, shaking off attempts at comfort and conversation. Over the ensuing months, she would come to feel comfortable enough to unburden herself, her thoughts and pain falling from her like misty rain. And always there was Ryan.

Why hadn't Brenton found a man like that? What was wrong with him? Did he have a neon sign on his head, a siren that called out to losers with baggage?

Months ago, when Christie had first talked about him, Brenton had listened and pictured Ryan: the dazzling edge of his jaw slightly bristly, his dark brown hair silky and slippery, and brilliant green eyes gleaming. When Christie had showed him a recent photograph from her phone, he'd been rigid with shock.

Ryan looked exactly as he'd imagined him.

"Cute, isn't he?" Christie had said with a smile as she dropped the phone back into her handbag.

"He is." Brenton had averted his eyes to focus on the small gray plastic bin under his desk. He'd stupidly printed out the profile of BlackTiger77 from the matchmaking site he'd checked out at lunchtime. Brenton had thought maybe he'd take the profile home to consider Mr. Black Tiger at greater length, only to belatedly realize the folly of his actions.

Christie's curls, a mix of blonde and brown streaks, swayed as she reached Brenton's desk. "See you Monday honey. I'd better go, apparently Ryan's home at a reasonable hour tonight." She smiled and, with a lift of her hand, turned for the door.

He wondered what he'd be doing tonight. Life was getting way too routine and he didn't feel like yet another evening at home watching a movie and eating pizza. He might head out to a bar on the weekend. It had been a while. Probably Roberto's.

Friday 18ᵗʰ January, 6.11pm

Connor was up and out of his chair and had just reached for his jacket when Ryan appeared from the door connecting the front public desk area to the rear office. The back office, reserved for sergeants and detectives, had thin brown carpet and desks of worn, dirty gray Formica. Cubicles of four were grouped together in the center. The exhaust fan rattled loudly.

"Connor, a quick word before you go?"

Connor threw his jacket back on the chair and turned to face Ryan. "Yeah, what's up? Happy to talk here?" Ryan was his almost son-in-law and Connor was careful to keep the boundaries between private and personal life as delineated as possible.

Ryan crossed his arms and bit at his lower lip. "It's about Gypsy."

"Yeah?" Connor searched Ryan's face for an indication of what was to come, but was stymied as Ryan put his head down and shifted his weight from one foot to the other.

"I know I've been skeptical and… well, what I'm trying to say is if it helps Christie, I'm willing to give it a go. She needs something and….er…"

Connor felt a surge of hope. Maybe, just maybe, they'd be willing to get to know and love Gypsy as he did. He knew Christie needed help but, stubborn as a mule, she wouldn't accept it, and definitely not from Gypsy. "How about dinner tomorrow night? No pressure, we'll take it as it comes." Smiling, he picked the jacket back up and headed for the rear exit, Ryan falling into step beside him.

Ryan stopped before the back door, the trenches on his forehead deepening. "Listen, mate, if I've caused offence, I'm sorry. It's the way I was brought up; we didn't go in for this kind of thing."

Connor put his right arm on Ryan's shoulder and gazed at him. Ryan examined the floor again before meeting his eyes.

"It's okay, I understand. Like I said no pressure. We'll see you tomorrow and see how we go."

"Thanks mate."

Connor headed back to the car park deep in thought. He'd automatically assumed that Christie would take to Gypsy the way he had, but they were like oil and water. Christie had been through a lot in her young life, and after losing a mother, father and brother, she couldn't see past her resentment. She'd been through hell in a relatively short space of time.

Hopefully they could all turn a corner Saturday night.

He whistled tunelessly as he unlocked the car and started it up.

Friday 18th January, 10.38pm

The evening out with Connor meant a great deal to me, as smack bang in the middle of an ongoing and intense investigation, he had arranged to take Friday night off. Connor was private as far as cops went. He mentioned cases but only in passing, and only when they reached the point, where they took over his life. The high profile murder case I'd been following in the news was one such case.

After a delicious meal at Sophia's—our favorite restaurant, with it being the venue of our first date and everything— the leisurely stroll all contributed to a relaxing evening which could only mean one thing. *Sleep.* My chronic insomnia meant I grasped at any opportunity for some shuteye.

Yawning when we arrived home, with the wine's soporific effect having taken hold, I headed straight for the bedroom. I didn't stop to undress, just dropped my handbag on the glass-topped table in the hallway as I passed it. Connor followed.

As I reached the end of the hallway, he lightly touched my hand and I turned to face him. His eyes had softened. Knowing Connor as I did, I recognized that look. He pulled me close, fingers burning through my blouse, reeling me in with his slow smile, his sweet breath tantalizing.

I examined the flecks of light green that his eyes showed when I stood close to them. He moistened his lips as he leaned closer to kiss me.

No matter how many times we had made love, my desire for him hadn't left—if anything, the more I learned about his idiosyncrasies, the more I loved them.

My fingers grazed his smooth-shaven cheek as his soft lips met mine. The kiss was initially slow and gentle. Then his mouth parted and a spark ignited as his tongue touched mine. I sighed and relaxed, my body melding with his.

The hairs on my arms and neck lifted and warmth spread throughout my body. Connor pulled me closer and he moved away briefly. His eyes, heavy with desire, raked across me greedily. I also craved his touch, needing more of him. My breath quickened and I arched back my head, letting out a sigh as his lips burned across my neck.

"Connor," I whispered, as he kissed a trail up my neck to just behind my ear. I moved my hands from his arms to his muscular back. Connor seemed chilled out, forgetting about work for a change. I ran my hands across his muscular shoulders.

I drank in the sight of Connor as he pulled his lips away to gaze at me, his swollen wet lips and hooded eyes telling me all I needed to know. He took my hand and gently led me toward the staircase.

As he stepped onto the bottom stair, the phone in his pocket rang loudly. A frown crossed his face.

"Ignore it," I whispered.

But Connor paused mid stride, hand to his pocket. With a sigh, he retrieved the phone to look at the screen. "Damn. It's the station. I have to get this, I'm sorry."

As I watched, he brought the phone to his ear. I couldn't believe it. I continued up the stairs and flung myself on the bed. Of all the rotten timing.

Connor remained on the stairs, where I could hear the deep rumble of his voice. The stair treads creaked beneath his weight before he appeared leaning against the doorway, face flushed. "I'm sorry."

"Me, too." I couldn't keep the longing out of my voice.

"If I wasn't in the middle of this damn case, I wouldn't worry, but…" Connor came to the bed and wrapped his arms around me. He kissed me on the lips— quickly, but still enough to make my pulse race.

"You better get out of here," I said and turned away.

"I'm sorry. I'll make it up to you, promise."

I didn't reply. I heard his footsteps on the stairs and the door closed behind him.

If I thought I had problems getting to sleep before, I didn't have a hope in hell now.

CHAPTER 2

Saturday 19th January, 6.21am

You have to stop him, Gypsy.

Net curtains billowed from the open window, the summer night beyond still and silent. Moonlight reflected off the lightly polished floors. The fragrance of lavender wafted in and I took a small step forward.

The bone-colored walls were empty except for a full-length mirror to my left. The room faded as my attention shifted to a wooden cradle in the middle of the floor, which creaked as it rocked, gently at first then building up to a rhythmic sweep.

Yet suddenly there was an unseen presence, unannounced but palpable. The sweet voice of a young girl spoke, echoing inside my head.

—You have to stop him.

This wasn't making any sense.

−I have to stop who? Who are you? What is this? I have no idea about any of it…

−I'm Isabella. It's Christie, she's in danger. He'll try to kill her.

−What? Who will? What are you talking about?

−She trusts him. She won't believe he'd ever do it, but he will.

My eyes snapped open. The light streaking through the edge of the blinds, by which I could see the stain in the corner of the ceiling, announced the beginning of another day. With the dream just behind my eyelids, I pushed myself up from the bed and thought about the voice of Isabella.

−That was weird.

So why this dream?

As an occasional telepath, I can tune into other people—usually the dead—pretty well, but never in dreams. Usually it happened as mind flashes or pictures while I was awake. This was a first. I'd always thought psychic mediums that received messages via dreams were just plain *weird*. Kind of strange coming from a telepath, I know, but there it was.

The last time I'd used my abilities had been a while ago, nearly a year in fact, other than occasional interchanges with Renee when we didn't want to share our conversation.

After Aaron, Connor's nephew, had not only tried to kill me in a hit and run but had also broken into my townhouse with the intention of torturing me as part of his screwed up payback plan, he ended up in a Melbourne prison and wouldn't be getting out for at least ten years. The justice system didn't take too kindly to cop killings, even if said cop was corrupt, as Connor's former partner Ian Robson most certainly was. I wondered if Christie visited her brother in jail, which might explain why we weren't the best of friends.

Connor and I had been together since our blind date. The strong connection we'd made on the fateful evening we met had been forged into something practically unbreakable, reinforced by his rescue of me when I'd needed him most. I loved our uniqueness. A psychic telepath with attitude, a detective with sentinel gifts who denied them, and regular dealings with death, either investigating murders or passing on messages from those that had passed on, meant our relationship was far from ordinary.

I heard the spray surging in the bathroom as Connor started a shower. I sank back into the warmth and security of my bed.

I closed my eyes for what felt like a moment or two but more likely minutes had passed. I sensed movement to my right, a faint rustle. Connor stood beside the bed dressed in a crisp white shirt, his chin up and hands fiddling underneath it as he finished tying a Windsor knot on a dark blue tie.

"Morning, gorgeous," said Connor, his voice a quiet rumble. A waft of spicy aftershave lingered.

I shuffled onto my right side to face him with a sleepy smile. "Hey, you. Big day, then?" The mattress gave way and crackled as he sat beside me.

"Another murder, possibly drugs related plus the intense Mr. Stinky case." Connor sighed and tugged at his earlobe. "I have to go, but I wanted to let you know: I invited Christie and Ryan over for dinner tonight." His gaze, like searchlights, almost burned my face as he gauged my reaction.

"Oh shit!" I bolted upright in bed and flung the covers off. "For god's sake, Connor, the place is a pigsty and I've got a full day of work today." I stood, running my hands through the bird's nest that served for bed hair.

"They're not coming to look at the place. They're coming for a reading for Christie." Connor stood at the door; his tight shoulders rose and fell. His edginess didn't surprise me. Whenever Christie and I were in a room together, the air could be cut with a knife. I needed to get to the bathroom and get rid of the stale taste in my mouth and he was standing in my way.

"A *reading*? Geez, Connor, I don't do readings. You *know* that!" I stomped toward him with the intention of reaching the bathroom. Connor grabbed my wrist lightly.

"Hang on lovely, hear me out."

I jerked my arm away and he released me.

"Connor, you know what I can do, but I don't do *readings*. What, does she think, I just turn on a psychic tap or something? Do you? Why the hell would Christie want a reading from me?" I rubbed the sleep from my eyes, glaring at Connor. Mornings were not the time for bad news.

He ruffled his damp blond hair. "I've talked to Ryan about it. We know they're both skeptics, but Christie is so desperate for comfort, for *something*, that she's agreed to see you, and Ryan has finally seen sense, if it will help her. She needs help and has finally agreed to it, sounds like. She wants to get in touch with Rae's dad…"

As I stomped toward the bathroom door, I snapped over my shoulder. "Great, thanks, Connor. A day of housework, work, and then tonight I get to prepare dinner for your desperate niece and her cynical boyfriend, both of whom are convinced I am a total fruit loop that has bedazzled you with my power. Fan-bloody-tastic." I slammed the door and turned the shower on. The hot water gushed and steam billowed up, a curtain of mist.

"I'll cook, promise," said Connor, his voice muffled through the bathroom door.

"Yeah, yeah, okay," I said, resentment pooling into a reservoir within my chest. Sprucing the house up for unexpected guests, especially Christie, who had tried her best but wasn't fully successful in containing her resentment, was not my idea of the perfect weekend.

As I soaped my wet hair, I tilted my head back and the smell of jasmine wound its way to my nose. I guess I understood Christie's resentment to some degree, but it didn't lessen the sting in its tail. She'd lost both biological parents at the age of twelve, first her father Dan, a cop killed in a courthouse explosion, and then her mother Rae had turned to the bottle for comfort and the house had burned to the ground the night she fell asleep smoking. Her aunt and uncle took Christie and her brother in as young teenagers, and then a couple of years ago Jill and Connor had split. So of course when I came along a year ago she was, well, I suppose 'reserved' was the best way of putting it. Then of course, her brother had turned out to be a psychopathic drug-addled stalker with a murderous bent and would spend the next decade in jail. Not much else in her life could go wrong. Overall, she had recovered remarkably well from the cruelty fate had dealt her.

Remorse stung. I realized I was probably too hard on Connor. I loved him intensely, but of course, when my grumpiness reared its irritated head, he was the closest and therefore most logical target. Maybe if I could be there for his niece and help her out, Christie and I could forge something closer, a real connection. I'd asked Connor if he and Christie had ever had the conversation he didn't want to face, the unspoken, festering secret. He hadn't told her he suspected he was her father, not her uncle. To be fair, how would anyone bring up something like that? It was simply too much, an ugly box of secrets that once opened could never be closed. Connor had been only eighteen when he'd attempted to console Rae, who was lonely because of her husband's long hours at work, and it had turned to a fit of passion. Christie was born nine months later. It wasn't my place to spill the beans, but the secret swelled within me occasionally, desperate to be revealed.

I stepped out of the shower and grabbed a towel, rubbing myself dry as quickly as possible. I needed to get dressed, eat, check emails, wrap up any work I had in record time and get stuck into sprucing up the damn living areas for tonight's farce.

***

Saturday 19th January, 10.14am

Christie relaxed her head back and gasped as the warm water ran down her body. For just a few minutes, she might be able to switch off the swirling ever-present thoughts. Switch off the pain, the torment, the tears, the constant searching and questioning. Why her grandfather, and why did the good people get taken? He'd been her rock in a sea of confusion. She'd been close to him and although her stepmother Jill had told her that he had terminal cancer nearly eighteen months ago, Christie had always assumed he'd pull through, tough old bugger that he was.

She remembered his strong arms, and how although he was in his seventies he still towered over her, and how a hug always made her feel safe, secure, buffeted for just a moment from the struggles of life.

After his death four months ago, she'd been numb. Somehow, she hadn't connected her grandpa with death. It hadn't clicked for her that he was gone. The unstoppable grief arrived in a flood about six weeks later.

When Christie had arrived at the church for his funeral, shuffling in with tentative steps, the hushed sanctity of the church and the sight of friends and family at the front pew had cracked open the dam of grief surging behind dullness. She'd told Connor that she'd like to view her grandfather's body, to say goodbye with happy memories instead of remembering him hooked up to machines in hospital. However, when the coffin was wheeled toward the altar, she'd splintered and broke, running from the church, face in her hands. It had taken every bit of self-control she had to return and sit calmly in one of the pews, tears streaming down her face.

At times, it didn't seem so bad; she got through the whole day without cracking up. Others, she was a mess, struggling to keep it together at work. She wondered if the grief would ever dissolve completely. Christie reached up for the conditioner bottle, squeezing and smoothing it across her wet hair. She arched her head back, eyes closed, suds flowing down her head and neck.

An unnatural weight amongst the water cascaded down the back of her head. She snatched

at it and brought her hand forward, lifting a clump
of gnarled matted hair to eye level. Her eyes
rounded and her forehead hit the shower wall.

"No, no," whispered Christie, her stomach a
mesh of nerves and terror as she struggled to stay
upright. The wooly snarling wreckage, the gnarled
knot of hair, signaled the end. She would end up
like Grandpa, hair falling out as he lost his fight
with cancer.

She gasped and headed out of the shower,
grasping onto the towel rail before her legs buckled
beneath her. She slid down the wall, her backside
thumping onto the bathroom floor. Christie fell
back. The ringing in her ears was so loud, so damn
loud. Burying her face in the towel, she fought to
get it together. Her pulse was beating hard and fast,
and her chest hurt, tight and burning. She had
cancer, she knew it. Ray's hair had fallen out then,
why else would hers be falling out now? *Oh, god.*
She took a slow, deep breath and blew it out slowly,
willing her heart rate to slow down. Levering
herself up along the wall, she snatched the towel
and wrapped it back around her body, flicking the
clump of hair onto the floor, eyes screwed shut and
mouth set in a grimace.

Damn it. The dam broke and warm tears
coursed down her face.

Christie yanked open one of the wardrobe doors,
crying and swearing quietly. If Ryan were here,
he'd help her get herself together. He'd been called
in to work again. But maybe that was the problem—

she was relying far too much on him. If she didn't get her shit together, he might start looking elsewhere. *Wouldn't he?*

He'd been her rock after her grandfather's death, his grumpiness giving way to support and caring, but the last few weeks he'd changed. The grumpiness intensified, had a sharper edge. He'd mentioned a serial assault case, Mr. Stinky due to victims reporting the attacker's vile stench, but she couldn't be sure if his change in demeanor was due to the ongoing case or a change of heart relationship-wise. She knew she didn't have her guard up at present, and doubted herself and the loyalty of those she loved more than usual.

Christie sighed and tugged at a couple of outfits in her wardrobe. She selected a few and threw them onto the bed, then rubbed the towel across her body so hard it hurt.

"Ouch!" she cried out, surprising herself, but the friction provided enough of a jolt to get her arse into gear. She stomped over to the drawers to rip out a set of underwear, sending the contents across the carpet.

She had to calm herself. Then she should ring up to book a doctor's appointment. She didn't know what she'd say, or if she could take more bad news. Maybe the day would get better.

Saturday 19th January, 6.29pm

Ryan had thought this would be a good idea, but driving to Connor's place he revised that decision. Deep in the thick of the so far unsolvable case, he wondered if his reserves of kindness were depleted. Battling traffic to visit a supposed psychic seemed like the last thing either of them needed.

As Ryan drove, Christie looked across at him, searching for a signal, a sign of what he might be feeling. Nothing. Her stomach was empty and her mouth dry. A horn honked behind them, and she gasped with a sharp uptake of the shoulders. Good grief, she was a nervous wreck. *It wasn't just her though; surely Ryan's hand shook slightly as he unlocked the car door?*

She wasn't sure why she hadn't told Ryan her hair was falling out. If she said it aloud, he'd think she was, well, flakey, nutty, completely losing the plot. Plus, now wasn't the right time. Things were too rushed. He arrived home an hour after she did and they had less than half an hour to get themselves changed and back in the car for the short drive to Gypsy's place.

"I'm nervous as hell." Christie kept her eyes on Ryan's profile and saw his cheek muscle tense.

He didn't take his eyes off the windscreen. "We don't have to do this, you know. We can change our minds. We have that right, Christie. Let's just have dinner and leave."

"No, I want to…well, I want to at least try. I might get to talk to Grandpa again one last time." Christie twisted her fingers before she looked back up through the windscreen. She'd been surprised when Ryan casually mentioned a possible reading from Gypsy; he was a complete skeptic and had been as long as she remembered. Whenever Gypsy's name was mentioned, he merely grunted. Hell, Christie wasn't sure about the woman or her abilities either, but if there was a chance, just a glimmer of hope she could talk to Grandpa even for a few seconds, it could change things for her. She knew it. It just might give her the closure she so desperately sought.

"Okay." Ryan blew out a long, thin stream of breath as the car stopped. He locked eyes on her. "You ready for this?"

His green eyes were as brilliant as ever. Christie wondered if there would come a time when they would be tired of each other, bored by each other. They'd been together for almost a year now and she loved him as much as she always did, if not more.

"Yeah, I think so." She tucked a lock of hair behind her ear.

The car had pulled up in front of Gypsy's small apartment in Carlton. Getting out, Christie breathed in the combined smells of a gardenia bush, light rain on concrete and garlic. Dinner would probably help loosen her up. She closed the car door, making eye contact with Ryan across its roof.

They linked hands and headed up the steps. At Gypsy's front door, they stood side by side, barely moving.

"Here we go," said Ryan. The door opened within seconds of the doorbell being rung.

"Christie, Ryan, come in." Connor's hair was slightly tousled and freshly dried and his shirt looked like he'd just thrown it on. Obviously, a big night, but then again, to Christie her uncle looked permanently disheveled, constantly rushing from one crisis to another.

Connor opened the door wide and smiled, taking a step back, gesturing with a welcoming extended arm they should come in. "Good to see you both. Come in guys."

Christie and Ryan walked through, their steps slow and tentative.

"Where's Gypsy?" said Christie as they reached the lounge room. Through the alcove between the lounge and cooking area, Christie saw Gypsy in the kitchen, clouds of steam surrounding her. She took a swipe at a strand of hair as she jammed the lid back on a crockpot.

"Oh, hi, guys," she said, wiping her hands on a tea towel. "Sorry I'm not more organized. But this wasn't my creation; I'm just taking Connor's pasta bake out of the oven. He's a man of many talents." Gypsy and Connor exchanged a brief look and

Christie and Ryan stood awkwardly in the middle of the small but cozy living area.

"Sit down, please" said Connor, gesturing toward the couch. "I'll get you both a drink—beer, wine? Something to take the edge off, I think." He bounded to the kitchen in long strides, swinging open a cupboard door to find the wine and glasses.

Christie and Ryan sunk onto Gypsy's purple couch. Ryan spread his arms along the back while Christie perched on the edge, chewing on her nails.

"I don't mind saying, I'm nervous as hell. I don't feel like eating anything." Christie was staring unseeing into a seemingly significant point on the floor.

Gypsy squatted down in front of her, their eyes meeting.

"Christie, me too, but you know what? I reckon we should try to eat a bit of something first, and then head into the study. Seriously, there's no pressure. We can just talk for a bit if that's easier…" Connor stood behind Gypsy, rubbing at his chest.

"Okay." Christie's face crumpled and her voice broke. "I'm sorry, I…" Her mouth contorted and she brought her hands up to cover her face.

Gypsy's hand rested lightly on Christie's forearm. "Come on, let's go. We can talk in the study."

Ryan pushed himself off the couch and was by Christie's side in a heartbeat.

"Let's go outside, mate, it's a warm night," said Connor. He headed toward the front porch, but Ryan remained fixated on Christie.

"Babe, are you okay?" He put one arm on her shoulder, but Gypsy had one hand on Christie's elbow, edging her toward the study.

"She'll be fine, Ryan, I promise," she said over her shoulder. "I'll take good care of her."

CHAPTER 3

Saturday 19th January, 7.01pm

My long-dormant mothering skills surprised me. Not that I think I'm an uncaring person, but when Christie opened up a crack and let the honesty flow I couldn't help myself. I turned to mush and the old hen in me began to flap its wings.

We sat around the desk in the study, Christie with head down and hair falling in her eyes. The combined smells of dust and paper and the familiar manila folders almost toppled off my desk. I moved one of the piles.

Despite Christie being curled in on herself, I grasped a clammy hand, willing her to come back from the depths of wherever she was hiding.

"Christie, honey," I murmured. "It'll be okay, I promise."

And there she was. *Holy shit.* Over Christie's right shoulder, I saw her. A child, a dark-haired figure, strands blowing across her face, eyes wide-open, arms by her side. Her stare didn't waver, her wraith like body a statue. Shit. Terrible timing. Whenever my ghostly visitors appeared regularly, I knew life would probably take a turn for the worse.

I knew in that instant that this was Isabella she was back.

Christie's head came up slightly and she spoke through a curtain of hair. "I know I've been a bitch at times, Gypsy, but sometimes it all hits me like a ton of bricks. It's too much. Dad, Mum, Aaron and now Grandpa. When will it end? Maybe Aaron's right and I'm too soft…"

With her left hand, she grabbed for the tissue box. She brought a tissue to her face and wiped her eyes. Scrunching it into a ball, she fumbled with a second tissue as she raised it to her nose.

Isabella had lifted a hand and was pointing at Christie.

−Tell her, Gypsy, tell her now. If you don't, she'll die and there'll be nothing you can do to stop it. Do you really want Christie's death on your conscience?

What the hell?

−Stop playing games, Isabella. Tell me who, how, when and where. Now.

I'd mastered the art of maintaining my composure and ensuring the living had no idea I was multitasking with the dead. While my focus remained heavily on Christie and helping her through this moment, the intruding voice of Isabella insisted, continued to pierce its way through my mind.

– Her hair has started falling out.

– What? Whose hair, Christie's?

– Yes. She's wondering if she has cancer like her grandfather Ray. She wants to talk to him but he's not here anymore, he's moved on.

Christie was looking up through her hair. I realized I hadn't responded to her.

"I understand, Christie. It's okay, you've been to hell and back these last few years. Aaron is wrong; you're not soft at all. Anyone would be devastated by what happened. *Anyone.* You're doing well, really well." I stroked the palm of her hand and was rewarded with the hint of a smile.

– You need to talk to her, Gypsy.

– Will you stop? Can't you see what's going on here? She's in pain, tormented, and I'm not going to talk to her about cancer or her grandfather unless she wants to.

– But if you don't warn her now she will be in agony, not just emotional but physical, too. The agony of death. Poisoning isn't pretty.

−You're being overdramatic. Who are you to us, anyway? Why are you here?

−I'll get to that. For now, you need to tell her: someone close to her is planning to get her out of the way, a slow poison.

−Who is this someone? Isabella, this is ridiculous. You know that, right? My relationship with Christie has always been dicey. I don't know how she'll take something like this. She'll probably never speak to me again.

−I can't give you the name of the murderer yet. He hasn't shown himself. But the intention is there. Do you want her to die? You can save her, warn her. Stop this now before it becomes anything at all.

−What do I do?

−Ray can't help here, he's moved on. It's about time Christie did, if she wants to save her own life.

As Christie warmed up and responded to my words and touch, the misty figure of Isabella faded.

Christie's chin jutted her red-rimmed eyes wide. "Is Grandpa here? Can he see me? Does he have a message for me?"

Here we go.

"I'm sorry, Christie, he's not here. Someone else was, though, and told me he's moved on."

Christie's head fell. "Okay."

"I need to talk to you about something else. It's very important." I leaned forward in my chair until my face was inches away from hers.

As she lifted her head, I saw how pale her face was. Under the desk light, I could see a light film of sweat forming on her upper lip.

"Has your hair been falling out?" I asked in a low voice. Now that it had been said, I couldn't unsay it. I knew the shit would probably hit the fan by my taking this on, but Isabella was right. If I didn't tell her, no one else would. My honor and integrity were more important than any potential fallout. Everything or nothing was now at stake.

Christie's mouth had fallen open and her hand was trembling beneath mine. She pulled it away and squeezed her eyes shut.

"How did you know?" she asked her voice shaky.

"The girl told me. I just got a message from her. She was here then she suddenly left," I said. I was second-guessing myself now. As it was, I was sensitive to the slightest ridicule as a telepath/psychic, paranoid about labels branding me a fruit loop and a nut, and had lost count of the number of times I'd copped smart-arse comments about what I do, even if I do it for love and not money. In this case, despite the suppressed resentment between us, my duty to Connor's daughter won out, even if she remained unaware of her paternity.

"Who is this girl? Does she know where grandpa went? Why is my hair falling out, does she know? Do I have cancer, too? I'm freaking out here." Christie lifted a shaking hand to her forehead.

Now was the time to break it to her. I took a breath and plunged ahead. "She seems to think someone is planning to poison you and wants you dead."

In a split second, Christie was out of her chair. "What the *hell* are you talking about? Poison? You're mad, completely off your trolley! This is *crazy*, complete bullshit." She sliced the air with her right hand as she spoke. Her eyes were cold and hard, and her nostrils flared.

"Christie, please. I didn't want to tell you, but if I don't, who will? Your life is in danger."

"From who*? You*? Seriously, I had my doubts and now I know why. You're a nutcase! I always knew you were jealous and wanted my uncle all to yourself, but I had no idea you wanted me out of the picture this much." The pitch of Christie's voice rose until she struggled for breath.

I stood up and reached out to her. "No, please understand what I'm saying. I've been told that someone that you love and trust will try to kill you. It was a warning, to prevent this from actually happening, a preventative gesture."

However, Christie became a wild colt, unbridled and making a bid for freedom from the tyrant that was her evil step aunt. She barged through the doorway and back toward the lounge room. I trailed behind her with a hand out.

"Ryan, let's go now." Christie's voice was hard and flat, its ominous edge slicing the air.

Ryan turned away from Connor and pulled hands from his pockets, reaching Christie in a few lengthy strides. As he hugged her, his stare flicked from Christie to me. I stood in the doorway, arms out.

"Christie, wait, this is a misunderstanding." I moved in an attempt to stand beside her, but she refused to look at me, powering ahead.

"You were right," she said to Ryan. "She's dodgy as hell, a manipulator. We were right not to trust her. Let's get out of here." Bounding through the front door and stomping down the steps, Christie headed for their car.

With round eyes, Connor rushed to the driveway where their silver Commodore waited.

"Hang on, Christie, what's this all about? What on earth happened in there?"

Ryan had already opened the car with the click of the remote, and he and Christie slammed into the car. It started with a hiss, and Connor watched from the driveway with feet wide apart, hands on his hips. Ryan gunned the car engine and then I heard the violent sharp screech of the tires as he slammed on the accelerator.

For a moment, Connor and I stood unmoving, and the street was silent other than a swish of trees and a hiss of possums.

A surge of energy shot through me until I was quivering and my limbs were tingling. Time stood still. I was squat in the middle of a worst-case scenario: Connor and I broke apart, and ridicule and scorn for me as a telepath. While my motives were pure, it didn't matter anymore. I should have said no to giving Christie a reading, no to telling her the truth about her hair falling out and the attempt on her life.

Our relationship meant more than this. Of course, Connor and I had been together a long time and been through a lot; but his good looks and the depth of my love for him meant there were times when my insecurities surfaced and I doubted my worthiness of happiness with a man who initially I'd thought out of my league. I mean how could a reckless, spontaneous, at times selfish woman, and a stunningly handsome man, stable, caring and infinitely patient, get together? Sometimes I wondered if my happiness would come crashing down in one fell swoop and Connor would laugh at me, telling me it had all been a practical joke.

It had happened so quickly, the situation spinning out of control before my eyes.

Connor had his back to me, facing the street. He turned in slow motion, hair flickering slightly in the wind. A small smile twisted across his face and he shook his head softly.

Oh god, this was it. I hadn't planned to put him in this position, but in that split second when I decided to tell Christie the truth about my vision, I had made a decision. A choice to sacrifice everything and stick my neck out to save her life. I'd seen how much Christie meant to him, more so than Aaron did, particularly as Christie was all he had left. Somehow, I knew if forced to make a choice again, he'd possibly choose family this time, not me. There could only be so much any person could take. A daughter didn't compare to a girlfriend of nearly twelve months, no matter how much he loved me. I should have stayed quiet. Maybe Christie might be in danger, but I wouldn't be facing the prospect of a life without Connor. Burning shards drove up within me and adrenaline surged.

My decision had forced Connor's hand and he was faced with a tough choice, not for the first time in our relationship. It wasn't fair to either of us, not the first time around and not this time either. He'd been forced to choose between his nephew Aaron and me a year ago, when Aaron had broken into my house and shot Connor's partner Ian. Connor had gone through hell, faced with a choice between family, love and morality. Love and morality had won, but I knew the ache of that decision stayed for longer than it should have.

I didn't want him to have to choose between Christie and I, but when it came down to it, that's what this was. I was terrified because I knew that Christie would win. Especially since he suspected she was his daughter, not his niece. I'd asked him months ago if he thought he would ever share his doubts with Christie, but Connor had simply lowered his eyes and turned away. I'd figured that was a no. What I didn't say was that it could backfire if she ever found out. I'd never tell her, of course, but there was still a risk.

Connor took two steps closer. He rubbed at the middle of his forehead. In the twilight, I could see the shadows under his eyes.

"What the hell happened in there?"

"Can we go inside? I need a drink before I say it out loud."

I headed back toward our home, trudging toward the front steps, each foot filled with lead. At the doorway, I took a deep breath and stepped in. As if our relationship hadn't been tested enough already, the ties that bound us were about to be stretched to their limit.

***

Saturday 19th January, 7.51pm

Leaning forward in the car seat, Christie sobbed. "Go, please just get us home."

Ryan waited for a moment for the sobbing to subside. "What happened, Christie? What did she do?"

Christie swiped a hand under her eyes. "I'm okay. Honestly, Ryan, I'm fine."

"Yeah," said Ryan. His fingers gripped the steering wheel tightly. "You need to tell me what happened."

"It wasn't what she did; it was more what she said. Grandpa wasn't there, he wasn't there!" Her eyes flashed and she moved a fist to her leg. She inhaled and Ryan swallowed, pushing the rising anger back down his chest.

"Okay. What did she say?"

A long silence, broken by a sniffle, and a sharp intake of breath the only response.

"Christie, what happened?"

"She said, she said…" Christie rubbed a tissue at her nose. "She knew my hair was falling out, and she said someone would try and poison me! She's full of it."

"Your hair's falling out? What?" Heat rose in his neck. "When did you think you were going to tell me?"

"It only happened this morning, and we were in a rush…"

Ryan was weaving through the chaotic Saturday night Carlton traffic and Christie grabbed onto the door handle with her left hand.

"Geez, Christie." He blew out a breath and swerved dramatically as a car suddenly swung out in front of them. He slammed the heel of his hand down on the horn and a long blast sounded. "Fucking idiot!"

"Ryan," said Christie with a warning tone, "calm down."

"Calm down? You're suffering stress, badly. You need to go to a doctor. There's that late night clinic we could go to."

"I'm a bag of nerves. My first thought was that I had cancer, just like Grandpa."

"No, Christie, it's stress. Losing hair is a symptom of chemotherapy, not fucking cancer."

The car had stopped at a set of lights.

Christie's tears slowed to a sniffle.

"So you don't think I have cancer, then?" She looked at Ryan. His face was red and a muscle in his cheek was twitching.

"No, I damn well don't!" he exploded. "If you'd told me your hair was falling out, I could have told you that." He stretched his fingers on the steering wheel.

"She told me someone would poison me. Someone I trust."

Ryan's lip curled as he sat back in the car seat. "So, what, you think I'm about to poison you? Is that what this is about?"

Christie didn't want to tell him that the thought had flickered through her mind, no matter how briefly.

The car pulled up in front of their flat, and they sat with the engine idling. Ryan refused to look back at her. He swallowed hard and shook his head, muttering under his breath.

After all this time together, were they having their first major argument?

"What are you doing? Turn the car off, let's go in."

Ryan slowly turned to face her. His eyes were dull and flat. "Get out," he said.

"What? Why, where are you going?" The hair on Christie's arms lifted and she froze, unwilling to move.

"I'm going out. Get out of the fucking car. Now," he growled.

Eyes round in shock, Christie pulled the door lever and elbowed the car down open. She stepped into the street and slammed the door behind her. Tires squealed, and with a belch of gray smoke, Ryan took off at speed. Christie stood on the footpath staring at the brake lights as the car stopped momentarily at the end of their street before the screeching tires of a right turn pierced her ears.

She swallowed hard and hung her head. After a moment, she headed for the front door, fishing in her handbag for keys as tears prickled her eyes. She wondered how he'd become so cruel in the space of twenty-four hours. Whatever was going on with him, she hoped he'd get the anger out of his system and come home in one piece. Soon.

***

Saturday 19th January, 7.41pm

Brenton saw Jake's face through the glass door as Jake pushed it open. Although the night had just begun, the place was filling up and the excited chatter of its patrons was building in volume. The blue walls, dimmed lights and stained wooden bar gave it an air of tired style. Although it had been quite a while since his last visit, Brenton knew he could relax here. He was amongst friends.

"Hey, cowboy," said Jake, his voice deep, and he threw one leg over the bar stool beside Brenton.

"I've told you, don't call me that," said Brenton, lips pressed together. He gave Phil the barman a nod and pushed his glass forward for more of the same.

"So what's the deal? I haven't seen you here in months." Jake turned his handsome blond face to Brenton. They'd enjoyed a fling a lifetime ago or more accurately about two years ago. They'd met at this very bar, and at first Brenton had been attracted to Jake's swagger, his blond slicked-back hair, the confidence and fake tan oozing from every pore. They'd gone home together and yes, it had been great, but after a few short weeks, Brenton realized it would never become a relationship. Jake was damaged, badly. Of course, most people were, but Jake's bravado and false persona simply didn't let up, and it wore Brenton down. He didn't keep contact with most of his exes, but Jake was another regular at Roberto's so he hadn't been able to avoid him. Once Brenton had explained that it could never go anywhere, Jake had been childishly resentful for a while, but they'd eventually settled back into a more relaxed friendship.

The bartender pushed another bourbon his way and Brenton thanked him with a nod and what felt to him to be a thin smile. He'd forced himself to come out, be sociable, get back in the land of the living.

"I haven't felt like it. I got used to my own company," he said, finally turning to acknowledge Jake.

"More like you settled for mediocrity. So how's middle class misery treating you?" asked Jake, flicking Brenton lightly on the shoulder with a grin.

"It's not that bad. Curling up at home with a DVD and a glass of wine doesn't mean my life is over." Brenton shuffled his bar stool toward his friend.

"Or maybe it means you've hooked up, and all you want to do is stay indoors." Jake winked and raised a beer to his lips.

"I wish. I've got my eye on someone, but it'll never happen. He's straight, for a start..." Brenton stared down into the murky brown depths of his glass.

"Oh god, don't start with the 'I can turn him' fantasy, please!"

"You think I'm not conscious of that? It's embarrassing enough admitting I'm in love with someone I've never met." Brenton spun away to sneak a look at the far corner of the bar where a young man and woman were giggling at a booth, arms entwined. At least someone might get lucky tonight.

"What?" Jake's voice rose. "How the hell can you be in love with someone you've never met? For real?"

"I didn't plan on it." A pinch of irritation crept in. "My mate Christie at work, she's had a really hard time since her grandfather died. She was unburdening. However, the more she told me about the ever-supportive and sometimes surly Ryan, how caring and sweet he was after her grandfather's death, well, I formed this image of him in my head. He's perfect, Jake."

"Oh my god, Brent, snap out of it!" With round eyes, Jake swung his elbow across the bar, poking his friend in chest.

"I wish I could," Brenton pouted, taking another slurp of his drink.

"You're gone, brother, you know that?" Jake asked his tone quieter now.

"I know." Brenton looked across the room. He realized his eyes were glazing over with tears and shook his head in a vain attempt to hide them.

"That's why I'm here," said Brenton, surveying his friend's face. "I need a distraction, to start focusing on other things. Something other than the perfect man."

"Well, I guess drowning your sorrows could work. For now." Jake raised his glass. "Here's to tonight."

Brenton raised his glass and managed a half smile. With a clink, they drained the contents of their glass.

CHAPTER 4

Saturday 19th January, 7.53pm

I threw myself down on the couch and blew out a breath. So far so good. Connor hadn't ranted and raved, and we hadn't broken up in a tearful exchange. Connor wasn't the type. He had years of practice at reining in his emotions, and that wasn't what I needed right now. I wanted to know what was swirling and burning inside that hunky body. He needed to spill, let me in to that sentinel mind of his.

He stepped in, his blond hair messy and shaggy, and moved through to the kitchen without looking at me, retrieving the abandoned bottle of wine. He poured two fresh glasses and faced me from across the breakfast bar.

"Connor, honestly I had no idea it would come to this. I had a gut feeling and I went with it."

His head went down and he picked up both glasses. In the lounge room, he sat next to me.

"Will you tell me what happened?"

"Yes." Although I was ready to tell him, my throat was constricted and my vision blurred. I faced him, eyes close to his. "I'm so sorry. I never meant to be the one to force a choice on you, not like this, never like this, I hope you know that."

His arms reached for me. I leaned my cheek on his shoulder as the warm tears gathered in the corner of my eye.

Connor's cheek rubbed mine gently. "I know you didn't. Neither of us could have planned this. We thought we were helping, and we both had the best intentions."

Relief washed over me. We'd stay together, but we were probably in for another bumpy ride.

"Can you tell me about it, lovely?"

God how I loved Connor Reardon in that moment. Enough to begin my story, slowly and tentatively.

"Friday night I had a dream, and I don't usually get spirits appearing in dreams, but I did for the first time for some reason. A young girl, Isabella, appeared to me that night. Earlier today, she warned me that Christie was in danger that someone was going to poison her. She must have really wanted to get in touch."

Connor's eyebrows knitted together. "Poison her? That's dramatic. But why?"

"I asked her that. She said she couldn't tell me yet. I don't think she knew. She said it would be someone Christie trusted and least suspected."

Connor's Adam's apple bobbed as he swallowed. "And that's what you told her earlier tonight. That's why we had that scene…" He was staring into thin air now, pondering on what this all meant, I guessed.

"Yeah. That and her grandfather wasn't here. Isabella said he'd moved on. She also told me Christie's hair had started falling out, and I don't think anyone else knew that, not even Ryan. It scared her." I ran my fingers through my hair. "I guess that's why she lashed out."

"She won't want to talk to either of us for a while, I'm guessing." Connor rubbed at his chin. "We should probably give her a bit of space."

"Yeah, considering she thinks I'm about to poison her, that's a good idea."

I rubbed Connor's knee. "I want to show you what happened. So you can see for yourself."

"What?"

"Tonight, when we go to sleep, come with me. You'll meet Isabella."

He lifted a hand. "Gypsy, no, I'm a sentinel, and a retired one at that. That sort of stuff is beyond me."

"How do you know? We have to at least try. Christie is your daugh—your niece. The family connection will help. How do you think Renee and I manage it? Please, Connor. For Christie's sake."

Connor rubbed the back of his neck and bit his bottom lip. "I don't know…."

I grabbed at his hand. "Just think about it, okay? We can give it a try later." The growling of my stomach told me it was time to eat the meal we'd slaved over.

"I don't know about you, but I'm going to reheat dinner." In the kitchen, I looked around at the abandoned food. I grabbed the casserole dish of pasta bake and shoved it into the microwave, setting it to reheat. I poured a glass of wine and found two clean plates. Connor had treaded over. He ran a hand down my left arm and the familiar tingle raced through me. I searched his face for any expression at all to get some semblance of what might be going on in there.

The pain reflected in his blue eyes.

"I'm sorry, Gypsy. Drama seems to follow us, doesn't it?" Warmth transferred from his hand on my back, burning through my light cotton top. I wrapped my arms around his shoulders and closed my eyes. My heart skipped a beat, grateful we were still together. Yet again, I'd doubted him, faced with a crisis forcing a choice between family and relationship; I still wasn't convinced of my place in his world. I had no reason to doubt him logically, but try telling that to my neurotic insecurities.

"It does." My mouth was inches from his. "But you know we'd be bored without it." I smiled and breathed in his sweet breath. I kissed him on the lips lightly, and as the microwave dinged, I pushed myself away from him. "Time to eat, I'm starved! Come on, let's eat, drink, and then hit the hay. Maybe we could take up where we left off last night."

Connor smiled as he took a plate and piled it with food.

***

Saturday 19th January, 9.29pm

I heard the buzz of my mobile phone. I grabbed it from inside my bra and entered my access number. It was a message from Leah.

"BBQ still on tomorrow at our place 1pm, be nice to catch up with both of you. Bring a salad or something?"

My mouth twisted at the irony of an everyday occurrence amongst the chaos of the Christie crisis. A barbecue on a sunny day. I texted her back. "Crazy here at moment, shit's hit the fan, but would love to come tomorrow. Will bring salad and check whether Connor is working."

Within seconds of putting the phone back inside its resting place, I felt it buzz and heard the muted ring. Leah was either concerned or curious as hell about what the crisis was, probably a bit of both.

I picked up the phone and swiped it, bringing it to my ear.

"Hi, Leah."

"Gypsy. What's going on?"

I tried to keep my sigh quiet and my voice as upbeat as possible. I wasn't fooling Leah, though; a sister is good at seeing through the façade.

"It's Christie. Connor arranged a 'reading' tonight and it didn't go well. She and Ryan stormed out earlier." I pinched the bridge of my nose.

Leah swore quietly. "What the hell is her problem? "

"I told her something she didn't want to hear."

"You're good at that." Trust Leah to tell it straight.

I sighed. "I had hoped for a truce. Wishful thinking I guess."

"Want me to come over?"

"Nah, I'll see you tomorrow."

Renee and Paul were murmuring in the background. "Well, you know where we are. See you then." Leah clicked off.

A barbecue would be a pleasant distraction. Roll on Sunday.

***

CHAPTER 5

Saturday 19th January, 9.21pm

Brenton took a long gulp of dark brown liquid from his glass. He gasped and slammed the glass back down onto the bar, his line of sight on the main entrance. A tall, well-built man with dark hair entered. A hand flew to his chest.

"Oh my god, that's him!"

Jake leaned closer to Brenton. "What? This is the guy? Are you serious?"

"What are the odds?" Adrenaline rippled through him, flooding his chest. This was his chance. It was a sign; destiny had quite literally opened the door for him. Now all he needed to do was walk through that door. A simple introduction should do the trick.

"I'm going over." He pushed himself up, but Jake put a hand out to stop him.

"Calm down, cowboy. Let's play this cool, real cool and slow. Probably a good idea to make sure you have the right guy first." With an arm across Brenton's chest, Jake nudged him gently back into his seat.

Brenton stared at Ryan, who had seen better days. The latter headed straight for the bar, with Jake following him with his eyes. Dark woolly stubble covered his cheeks and chin, and eye sockets set back in his skull. Ryan ordered from the barman, glaring at an older man who had jostled him.

"So what's the plan then, Einstein?" asked Brenton.

"We watch and we wait," said Jake, taking another drink. "We've got all night."

***

Sunday 20th January, 12.58am

"I think that's enough," said the bartender, placing a firm hand over Ryan's glass.

He slouched over the bar, swaying, almost falling off the barstool. He raised his lolling head to scowl at the barman.

"Another drink, please." His speech slurred but Ryan barely noticed, nor did he seem to care.

Two men appeared at his side, blond, fit, tanned and looking like something out of a magazine spread. *What did they want?*

"It's okay, Phil, we'll take it from here."

"I hope so. Otherwise, security can sort it out."

With protests from Ryan, they grabbed him under each arm and headed for the door. Once outside, he promptly stopped protesting to throw up in the gutter.

*****

Sunday 20th January, 3.56am

By four in the morning, Christie verged on hysteria. Ryan didn't stay out this late, he just didn't. Gruesome images of his body, twisted and bloodied inside his smashed-up car, pushed their way into her mind and wouldn't leave no matter how she tried.

She'd gone to bed, hopeful that eventually she'd be off in the land of nod. Sleep had evaded her, with her just kicking and tossing in bed. In the end, she'd sat up on the edge, staring at the wardrobe door, worry and anxiety eating away at her.

She thought about calling the police station, the hospital, or both. The only issues that held her back were potential embarrassment of Ryan and he would react to that. The thought of bothering Ryan or his colleagues with a needless call horrified her in his present mood. How could she explain to them that something had really happened to him, this wasn't like him at all. They rarely went out, and spent most of their time together. Ryan rarely, if ever, stayed out all night. They were usually only apart for a night shift, never socially. In the eleven months they'd been together, he'd never stayed out this late, ever. Something bad had happened to him, she knew it.

Pushing herself up from the bed, Christie headed for the kitchen, where she reached for the telephone with blank eyes. The dial tone sounded as she pushed the green button and she stared at the phone before bringing it to her ear. After speaking to an operator, she wrote down the number of the local hospital. When the receptionist answered, she realized the stupidity of what she was doing. She was overreacting; of course he was fine; they would laugh about it together once he got home. The hospital staff would think her a complete nervous wreck.

Shit.

Apologizing profusely, she explained the situation and was put on hold briefly. The woman at the front desk was all business, and asked for Ryan's details. No, he wasn't there, and hadn't been admitted. Christie hung up, wrung her hands and made her way back to the darkened bedroom to recommence her vigil.

***

Sunday 20th January, 9.37am

Ryan's eyes fluttered and opened to slits. He sucked in a breath and sat up quickly, his eyes flying all the way open. Where was he? He was naked and in an unfamiliar bed, not a good combination. Ryan swung his legs to sit on the edge of the bed, desperately trying to recall events of the previous night. Judging by the bitter taste in his mouth and the pounding in his head, it involved substantial amounts of alcohol.

He recalled the scene at Gypsy's, then storming out and leaving Christie by the side of the road. He rubbed at his gritty eyes. What the hell had he been thinking? Why did he leave Christie like that when she needed him more than ever? He cringed. He couldn't believe he'd done that to her. Ryan pushed up from the bed and pulled a sheet around his naked body. His clothes must be around here somewhere. He spotted the entranceway to a bathroom and headed toward it.

Surely, he didn't go home with someone last night. Shit, he knew he wasn't perfect, but he knew without a doubt that he hadn't done anything like this before. He didn't have a track record of playing up on Christie, or anyone else for that matter. Or did he? The pounding hangover had messed with his head.

The sheet swished behind him as he moved from the bathroom through the bedroom to the hallway, where he saw what looked to be a kitchen through another door. An immaculately groomed young man was at the bench, preparing breakfast.

"Well, good morning handsome, remember me?" he said with a lazy smile.

His head was killing him. "Who the hell are you?" Ryan pulled the sheet tighter around his waist.

He slowly approached Ryan, one hand out to touch him but Ryan snapped his arm away from his semi naked form. "Fuck off! What the hell is this?"

"I'm Brenton. Breakfast?" said Brenton, raising his eyebrows. Ryan's outburst barely ruffled a feather.

Then Ryan remembered last night at the bar. This guy was there. So was another one, Jake. Ryan had been drunk, very drunk, completely smashed, in fact. It dawned on him slowly at first, a prickling fear crawling up his spine, then an ache at the back of his throat. *No, no, not this.* He'd do anything, anything, but not this, surely.

He lurched toward Brenton, grasping for his neck but failing to make contact when Brenton pushed him away. "You! You fucking prick! You brought me here. What are you, some kind of faggot?"

Brenton heaved forward, struggling against Ryan, pushing him away before he could get hold, and Ryan stepped back, panting loudly.

"Hey, calm down, what do you think this is? I helped you. You were paralytic, completely pissed, about to collapse. I dragged you out of the bar, got you in a cab and brought you home. You didn't seem to mind at the time," he added, eyes wide.

"I was off my face, you fucking parasite!" Rage boiled and Ryan rocked back on his feet, waiting for the opportunity to knock Brenton into oblivion. He however, simply walked away.

Ryan clenched his fists as his chest burned, the rush blinding him. He headed back to the bedroom to find his clothes. He needed to get out of here, back to Christie. Had he really betrayed Christie? If so, why now? They'd been together a long time. He didn't remember the sex, nor did he remember consenting. Did he enjoy it? Given the raging hangover, he doubted it. If he did go along with it, what did that mean? Did he prefer men? Women? Hell, it confused him.

Sure, he might have got drunk in a bar, ridiculously drunk, which was damn stupid in itself. However, going home to sleep with a man? Hell, he wasn't that way inclined drunk or sober. Did he have it in him to risk his relationship with Christie and possibly his career for a night of drinking and sex with a random stranger? No, he didn't, he was sure of it. So how did he end up here?

He must have been completely wasted.

Reaching the bedroom, Ryan searched for his clothes, which he found in a crumpled pile at the bottom of the bed. Dressing in a hurry, he scanned the room for his keys, wallet and phone. Where did he leave his car?

Think, Ryan, *think*.

The furious drive from Gypsy's place came back to him, how he'd driven with no direction until he ended up at the bar. Roberto's in Brunswick. He'd parked the car round the back. Shoving his feet into shoes, he wriggled his feet until they were in. He stormed back to the lounge room to find his stuff. He didn't want to talk to the person in the kitchen. The situation was already a disaster; he didn't want to make it worse by losing his temper and smashing someone's face into a million pieces. He needed to get out of there, and fast.

As Ryan began to lift cushions on the couch in a vain search for his keys, he felt Brenton's presence behind him. Ryan turned and glared at him.

"Looking for something?" The expression on the man's face was guileless, without a trace of aggression.

"Yeah, my fucking stuff. Keys, wallet, phone, where did you put it? I'm outta here." Ryan's hands were on his hips. Brenton was taller than him and bigger, but Ryan knew he could take him on and break a nose or knock him out if he had to. It would probably be the only way to keep this dickhead quiet.

"I've got those, they're safe." Brenton wiped his hands on a tea towel and smiled without a hint of malice. Ryan, however, knew better.

"Look, if you give me them now, I won't say any more about this. I'll keep quiet and won't make a fuss. No need to press charges." Ryan had found his confidence, certain of regaining his equilibrium and salvaging the situation.

"Press charges? I didn't kidnap you, if that's what you're thinking. You didn't seem to mind at the time. I'll never forget last night, ever."

Ryan took a step toward Brenton, pointing a finger at him. "Let me make this clear. I love my girlfriend. Last night never happened." Ryan scowled "Why didn't the taxi drop me home?"

Brenton took a step closer. They were standing in the archway between the lounge and hallway, where the floor switched from carpet to tiles. In a heartbeat, Ryan had calculated how long it would take to get Brenton on the ground and crack his head open like a watermelon.

"Actually, you were beyond speech at that point. I was about to check your wallet to get your address from your driver's license, but after you vomited all over it I wasn't so keen." Brenton's hands were by his side, his nose screwed up in disgust.

Rage surged through Ryan. "I am not what you think, not what you want me to be. You and I did not happen, simple as that. I love my girlfriend, end of story. Give me my stuff. Don't make me get a restraining order. The sooner I'm out of here, the better."

Brenton sighed with such force that his shoulders heaved. It wasn't going to happen as he'd imagined. Did Ryan feel anything for him?

He approached Ryan, one arm outstretched. "Look, I think there's been a misunderstanding–"

Ryan's teeth clenched his muscles rigid and eyes popping. "Get my fucking wallet, keys and phone. *Now*."

"All right," said Brenton quietly. He went to the kitchen and opened the top cupboard, which held the items. Returning to Ryan, whose face was turning from purple to red, he handed them over.

"If you change your mind, you know where I am. I'll be here, waiting." Brenton's voice was almost a whisper.

Ryan snatched his things from Brenton's outstretched hand.

"And if I ever hear a word out of you, you'll be sorry. Don't think of that as a threat, it's a fucking promise." He stormed toward the front door, swung it open and slammed it behind him so loudly that it vibrated on its hinge.

***

CHAPTER 6

Saturday 19th January, 10.03pm

Well, all right, I'll give it a go, but only for Christie's sake," Connor said as I packed up the dishes after our far too eventful night. "How does it work?

I dropped my tea towel on the bench and turned toward him, inches away from his sweet breath, and ran my hands down his arms. The blond hairs on his forearms were soft yet masculine.

"Renee and I set a connection with touch," I murmured, and his magnetic blue eyes locked onto mine. "We always hold hands. That cements the bond, and we take it from there. I'm hoping we can do the same and you can come with me when Isabella visits. How do you feel about cementing a bond?" My lips curled into a smile as his hands found their way to the back of my waist. The warmth spread from the small of my back to my shoulders and neck, and I shivered.

Connor kissed me, his mouth wet and warm. My arms slid around his neck. After all this time, despite nearly a year of togetherness, he could still do it for me. It was always him, no one but him.

His fingers brushed my cheek as he pulled away. "Let's give it a try, then, and see where we end up." His expression had relaxed—although the trenches under his eyes were dug deep, the tension seemed to be leaving him.

"I'm going up." I gazed at him, lust slowly transforming me, and I moved away slowly with a last touch of his hand before heading upstairs.

I assessed my bedroom. Thankfully, most of the time I forgot that this room was the scene of two shootings and more than a bit of torture.

It didn't look the same. Before Christie and Ryan's visit, I'd finished a mad flurry of tidying up which had spread to my bedroom. I'd picked some flowers out of the garden and they were sitting on the windowsill in a jug, the dark night behind them. My clothes were picked up and dumped in the laundry basket and the bed had been made for a change.

The perfect scene for romance, and a journey into the unknown.

In the bathroom, I showered quickly, cooling down from the warm weather and refreshing myself.

I pulled back the blankets and groaned as I landed in the softness of my bed, relaxing as it molded to the contours of my body. I hoped Connor wouldn't dawdle, and sure enough, before long I heard a creak on the stairs.

He stood just inside the doorway, looking down at me, his face grave. He began unbuttoning his shirt and I settled in to watch. Watching Connor undress was one of life's pleasures.

"Gypsy, this isn't going to make things any worse, is it?" His eyebrows moved closer together.

"I don't know how it can get any worse—other than something happening to Christie, that is. Unbelievably, that's why I've stuck my neck out. I know what she means to you, and I couldn't live with it on my conscience if any harm came to her."

"I know that." Connor was down to his underwear and I struggled with distraction.

The bedspread lifted as he slid in beside me. "I wonder if she'll ever appreciate what we're doing for her," murmured Connor. As I lay on my side, the vibrations of his deep voice reached me.

Connor draped one arm over my hip. "Does it matter that I'm a sentinel, not a psychic? I can block readings—the few times I did anything, anyway. A sentinel protects and guards, I don't go looking to make contact."

His hair was damp, and I ran my fingers through it gently. "Necessity is the mother of all invention, honey. I'd never tracked a living person down using my powers before Aaron decided to hunt me down, but I did it. If Christie's life is in danger, we can do it again."

As I kissed him softly, I became aware of a shadow, a presence in the far corner.

Shit, Isabella has rotten timing. She could have at least waited an hour or two until our romantic interlude was over.

"She's here," I whispered. Connor's head lifted off the pillow, his neck corded and strained as he searched the room for her.

"Take my hand," I whispered to him. His eyes went round and he swallowed hard. As he brought a hand up and out of the coverings, I took it. "Come with me, Connor—quickly, now."

His fingers linked with mine, and I sat up in bed. I saw her standing patiently at the bottom left corner of the bed, face unsmiling. She looked to be eight, maybe nine years old, and her dark hair hung straight and heavy.

—Isabella, I'm glad you're here. I brought someone with me.

—I see that. It's been a while since I met a sentinel, Christie's father.

Connor's face changed color. He surveyed the room until his eyes fixed on the spot where Isabella stood. He'd found her.

His fingers were still intertwined with mine. His deep voice, nervous and unsure, rebounded through my mind.

—Er…Isabella. How is Christie? Who is this murderer?

—Don't worry, she's fine—for now. She's freaked out, but that's to be expected. Gypsy's info really threw her. Give her time to make sense of it. Right now, she's coping with Ryan. He's disappeared.

—Ryan? Is he the killer?

—I don't know yet, all I know is that someone close to her wants her out of the way. I've tried parting the curtain, but he hasn't revealed himself yet. Soon though, soon. As soon as he reveals himself, I'll be in touch. Find him and stop him.

Connor had sat up on the bed now, muscles tensed in a way that revealed his every nerve on high alert.

—Ryan wouldn't do this, he wouldn't. I've known him for years.

—Like you knew Ian Robson? Isabella seemed harsh in her directness.

The thick silence seemed to go on for a long time.

—Point taken. Nevertheless, I don't think Ryan is capable of this. I need to go to Christie and find Ryan. If I take some time off, I can protect her.

—Not this time. Your paternity will become an issue, though.

I cringed. Isabella had no boundaries, and said what she believed needed to be said. She didn't sound like any nine-year-old I'd met before. I couldn't be sure of Connor's reaction; as usual, he gave away little. An instant later, he squeezed my hand and met my gaze. As I'd telepathically communicated nothing in the conversation, I wondered if my thoughts were automatically transmitted via the three-way link.

—How? I'm not convinced I am her father...

—You are, trust me on this. If she ends up in hospital and needs a blood transfusion or an organ transplant, be ready.

—If I have anything to do with it, things won't get that far.

I hadn't said much, I'd left most of that to Isabella but then I wanted Connor to see and hear her. I'd taken a back seat deliberately.

—I know that. Right now, the best thing you can do is convince her to be on alert. That includes monitoring her food and drink.

Connor flung back the bedcovers and was up and out of bed.

With a snap, the connection was broken. Isabella didn't move.

—Gypsy, don't let him go. It will make things worse. I don't know if either one of them will believe this until it happens, I'm afraid. They have to believe you're a kooky weirdo, all of this flies in the face of their indoctrination, false information. Believing in the spirit world is too confronting. Ryan's parents convinced him spirits don't exist,

and he's brought Christie round to his way of thinking. Call her or get a message to her somehow. But don't go and see Christie tonight. She's struggling and not in the right frame of mind. Connor can talk to Ryan at work tomorrow. As soon as I see the killer, I'll be here. You'll be the first to know, or at least a close second.

And with the trace of a smile, she was gone.

I bounded out of bed to close the wardrobe door, where Connor was ripping clothes out.

"Stop, Connor, stop!" I grabbed his hand. "No!"

He paused, holding a pair of shorts ready to get dressed. Hair fell in his eyes as he looked up at me. "I have to go. She needs me."

Were those tears forming in Connor's eyes, or simply sweat? In nearly a year, I'd rarely seen Connor cry, despite some of the worst experiences a person could go through.

I fastened my grip on his hand and moved closer. "You heard what Isabella said. We could make things worse. Come to bed, honey. Leave it." My voice was soft and soothing, as if to a child. I struggled with the urge to hold him in my arms and rock him to sleep.

I pulled at his arm and slowly he followed. "Come to bed, babe. You can talk to Ryan in the morning. Life is always better with sleep. Come on."

Connor was mute, and as he fell onto the bed obediently, I held his head to my chest and rocked him, just as I'd wanted. I drifted into sleep, contented and grateful that Connor was with me. Yes, we were in a boatload of trouble and the waters would more than likely get stormier, but tomorrow was a new day.

***

Saturday 19th January, 10.31pm

Renee had been lying in bed when the unexpected breeze blew across her skin. It was on. Again.

She needed to talk to Gypsy urgently. She'd tried to establish a link a couple of days ago but it wasn't the right time. Gypsy was stuck in the middle of a crisis, yet again. After extending her abilities almost a year ago when that bastard had tried to kill her aunt Gypsy, she hadn't needed to use them again. On Friday night, her abilities had reawakened. A little girl had appeared. At first, she'd thought she was imagining it. But she wasn't.

Renee had just put her book away to hunker down and sleep when a strong breeze blew across her cheeks. There were no windows open and no fans in the room. As she sat up, she sucked in a breath. A dark-haired girl with a serious expression stood at the bottom of her bed.

She looked to be about eight or nine, a deep frown marking her face. Then it began.

−Renee.

Renee rubbed at her arm. *−Who are you?*

−A friend. My name's Isabella. I'm here because I need your help. To save a life.

Weren't they always? Spirits had never appeared to wish her goodnight. Renee didn't want to get involved in any more messes from unknowns that needed help. Because of the previous nightmare, Gypsy had nearly died and Mum practically had a nervous breakdown.

−I know all about the trouble you had with Aaron. But this is different.

Renee's stomach tightened. This girl could read her thoughts as soon as they occurred, and she didn't like it one bit.

−Different how? I don't want to get involved. Last time, things got nasty, really nasty.

−I know that. A woman is about to be murdered and you can help stop it.

Murdered? That confirmed it. This was way over her head. She wasn't even fifteen yet, far too young to involve herself in capturing criminals yet again.

−It's Christie, Connor's niece. Someone will try to poison her.

−So why me? Gypsy can help I know she can.

−I've talked to Gypsy. She tried to help by giving Christie a reading, but it's spiraled out of control. Christie overreacted. She doesn't believe her and now she thinks Gypsy is out of her mind, or

a fraud. Christie won't listen to either Connor or Gypsy now, probably not until it's too late. But Christie might listen to you.

—What? Christie, Connor's niece, you mean? She doesn't know me, and I'm only a kid. If you tell Gypsy who the murderer is, she'll stop it. She did last time, even when her own life was in danger. I trust her. You should, too.

—I do trust her. But Christie and Ryan won't listen, and as soon as I tell Gypsy and Connor who the murderer is, I'm worried hot heads will rule. It could get nasty. I want you to talk to Gypsy about the murderer's identity.

—What? I still don't understand.

Life had been good for a long time now, and Renee was enjoying it. Dad had moved back home and, other than the odd argument; he and Mum were getting along fine. Some people might have said her life was boring and routine, but Renee liked it just as it was, thank you very much.

—All I'm asking you to do is talk to Gypsy. I've told her, but she needs to understand that Christie's killer is planning her murder. Soon. It looks like it's someone at her workplace, not Ryan, her boyfriend.

—How can you tell? How do you see him? What's going on in there?

—You mean the spirit world?

—Yes. How and when do you know?

Isabella paused for a moment.

—It's hard to describe, the two worlds are vastly different. Imagine a long dark tunnel. As you journey down the tunnel, entrances to rooms are carved into the side. Each is covered with a curtain. I don't venture into the tunnel or one of the rooms unless something alerts me, a knowing, and an instinct, intense emotion from the living. I got an alert from Christie.

A light prickle began its way up Renee's back.

—Why are you watching her.

—I'll keep that quiet for now. The information is on a need to know basis, but you will, in good time.

—So how did you see him?

—Through a parted curtain, flung back. My world is similar to yours in some ways, but we pay more attention to instinct. Instinct took me to Christie's workplace. The more real and solid his plans become, the more I see of him. Now it's barely a thought, a flicker, a murderous intent, but it is there. He hasn't worked out the how yet. I don't think he's fully convinced himself of what he will do or how he will do it. His mind is dispersed. I know he works with Christie because when I part the curtain there she is, and I hear a man's voice. But that's all.

Renee's pulse skipped into high gear. *—Well, I'm sorry I can't be involved in something like this again. Last time, Gyp was nearly killed.*

—But did you have someone like me watching and guiding you last time? I'll take care of you, I promise. No harm will come to either of you.

Renee tugged at the pendant around her neck.

—Well, maybe. I'm seeing her tomorrow.

—Good, it's settled. I'll get in touch again soon.

Like a bird, the girl took off almost as if she had flown away.

Renee's stomach lurched, as if it had been wrung out and twisted. She turned over in bed, attempting to get back to sleep. Where this would lead them she didn't know, but she hoped this time they would be safe.

***

CHAPTER 7

Sunday 20th January, 10.16am

When I awoke the next day, Connor was gone. I reached out to touch the place where he'd slept. It was cold. He must have been gone for a while, but then I knew he was working today, an early start at the station.

The fluorescent numbers on the alarm shocked me. I couldn't remember the last time I'd slept in, even on a Sunday, but then I'd tossed and turned until the early hours of the morning when I'd succumbed to sleep.

I groaned as I levered my body out of bed and headed for the shower. There would be a barbecue at Leah's place today and I looked forward to seeing Renee. It had only been ten days since I saw her, but it felt like an eternity. We had always been close, but then sharing a telepathic bond would do that for blood relatives, regardless of age.

After dressing quickly, I headed downstairs to find my phone. I found Leah's number and gave her a quick call.

"Gypsy? What's happening? You still coming?"

"Yeah, I'll just make a quick salad then I'll come over."

Leah sounded relaxed and happy, a pleasant change after our conversation the day before. "Renee is desperate to see you, of course. But it's a low key affair, just us and you so far."

That was exactly the way I liked it. I'd already let the light in by raising the blinds and it looked like a warm summer day, and a casual breath of routine family functions was just what the telepath ordered.

I hadn't told either Renee or Leah that I planned to make a visit either before or after their place. Hell, I couldn't be sure myself how I'd be received, and there was only one way to find out.

I signed off from my conversation and after whipping up a quick salad, I was out the door.

In the car, I mused over what the day might bring. I'd already sent a quick SMS to Connor, asking him to let me know the lay of the land once he'd spoken to Ryan. Hopefully, the drama had died down and Paul and Leah were back to happy families.

Renee, as far as I knew, had no dramas in her life, a refreshing change for a teenager. At least *someone's* life was free from drama. Then, she was only fourteen; there would be time for drama later. I pulled into the driveway of their home and headed in. The front door was open and the tantalizing smell of meat sizzling on a barbecue grill wafted in.

I made my way through the front passageway toward the back yard, the sound of laughter ringing through the hallway.

As I reached the door to the back patio, there was Leah, her brown hair tousled, skin glowing, a smile written across her face.

"Gypsy!"

Leah was carrying a couple of glasses, which she put down on a bench before reaching across to kiss me.

"Come through! The usual gang is here." Leah strode ahead.

"Everything okay with Paul?" I wanted to slip the comment in before we reached the patio. I didn't want to be the tipping point for another family drama.

"Oh, that…" Leah turned to me, her face coloring slightly. "Look, I should have waited before I called you. I was still in the thick of it. It was all over before it began."

"So you never heard from Rita again? All good on the marriage front, then?"

"Yeah, she won't be back, not after having the door slammed in her face. I believe Paul when he says he knew nothing about it—how could he? There has to come a point where I trust him again."

Fair enough. As we reached the doorway, I heard Renee's running feet clatter on the tiles behind me. I turned and she ran toward me with bright eyes and arms outstretched, which she threw around me. She'd grown. Her arms reached my armpits rather than my waist.

Had she grown in ten days? We were so close, and ten days seemed like a long time. How did I not notice something like this in someone so dear to me? I needed to see her more often.

"No, Gyp, I haven't grown that fast. You need to pay more attention." She grinned and patted my shoulder—"I have missed you, though"—and she squeezed me. As she did, I saw the flash, thunderbolts cracking open with the connection.

—I need some time with you urgently. Isabella paid me a visit.

I smiled at Renee, remaining composed, as I'd done often enough.

—Okay, just let me spend a bit of time with your mum. Then we'll catch up somewhere quiet.

Well practiced in the art of business as usual, I released my grip on Renee and followed Leah, who collected some salad dressing from the fridge before stepping outside. Renee stepped away, I assumed to hang out in her favorite place, her bedroom.

"So what's the latest?" I asked Leah as we sat on two lawn chairs a couple of meters away from the barbecue. "Other than your visit from dragon lady, that is."

"Actually, Paul's got a new job." Leah leaned back in the chair, the sun hitting the highlights in her hair.

"He has? What kind of job?"

"Promotion," said Leah, pulling down her top and rearranging it. "He's a site manager now, seems to be enjoying it. I'm enjoying the healthier pay packet, that's for sure. Definitely takes the pressure off."

I was genuinely pleased for Leah. After everything they'd been through, things were finally looking up for them.

"So all good then?" I asked, reaching inside my handbag for a pair of sunglasses.

"As good as any marriage can be, I guess. I'm starting to trust him again, and we almost like each other. There's even the odd moment of affection." Leah took a sip of the cool drink beside her.

"I'm pleased to hear it. I bet Renee is, as well."

"Yeah. She seems to be doing well at school, which is great. It's nice to be back to a routine after the hell we went through last year." I wasn't sure if Leah was referring to her marriage's near-breakdown, or the fact that I'd almost been killed. Possibly a bit of both.

Renee poked her head around the corner and joined us on the back patio, pulling up a chair beside us.

"What were you doing?" I said. "Hiding upstairs?"

Renee smiled. "Nah, I figured you wanted some time with Mum." She certainly didn't seem patient though, judging by her foot tapping on the tiles.

Renee flashed me a look.

"Let's eat," I said, rising to stand next to Leah, who strode in front of me, making her way to the barbecue. Renee and I followed. I thought I heard her hiss something at me under her breath, but decided she would have to wait, no matter how much I loved her.

The sun, the garden and laughter washed over me. Paul turned meat at the barbecue. I reached over to kiss him on the cheek.

"Hello, stranger," I said. "Good to see you again." Paul turned his tall, lanky frame from the barbecue and gave me a brief smile.

"Hiya. Glad you could come. Burger?" He gestured toward a platter of grilled meat.

I picked up a plate. "Thanks. I hear you got a promotion, nice one."

"Yeah," he said, concentrating on transferring meat from the barbecue to the platter. "I've got a new company car coming. The dealership has ordered it in. It's nice to be appreciated."

I smiled up at him. "I bet. This just proves that sometimes good things really do happen to good people."

"Thanks." He flashed me a grin.

"Excuse me," I said. "I'm going to eat, then catch up with my niece. Thanks for this." And with a wave of the hand, I headed back to my seat.

Leah was sitting down, eating already. "For god's sake, Gypsy, will you put Renee out of her misery after you've eaten? She's like a cat on a hot tin roof, desperate to talk to you. I think it's one of those 'things' again." Leah flicked a warning glance at me. "I hope there won't be trouble this time and you won't involve Renee in things she shouldn't be a part of. If she cries, you cry."

I focused on the food on my plate, shrugging. I understood Leah's worry well enough. During the crisis last year, Renee had been my voice, and I'd enabled our connection, where she'd spoken to Connor while I was laid up in hospital, and he'd investigated and rescued the abducted woman. In the course of the mayhem, Aaron had tracked Renee down and followed her home from school. Leah practically flayed me alive when she found out.

I waved Renee over. "Have you eaten?"

"Yeah. Can we go inside and talk?"

"Just give me a minute." I grabbed my bag and placed my hand in Renee's. She immediately turned and led me back inside. The girl was impatient, that was for sure. We reached the lounge, which was darkened and quiet.

"Sit down, Gypsy. It's important." Her frown and her hand tightly clasped gave me an indication of what was to come, although Renee had always been a serious child.

I sat in the soft, dark pink armchair and rested my arm beside her, palm up. With a hint of a smile, she nestled her hand in mine.

"Let's go," she said.

I knew whatever she was telling me must be confidential. For nearly a year now, we hadn't needed to speak telepathically. Life had been refreshingly quiet.

−Isabella came to see me last night.

−So you said. I have to admit I'm surprised. Why would she do that?

−She said things are getting pretty heated between the four of you. She wants me to speak to Christie.

−What? That won't be happening; I don't need your mother on the warpath again, screaming at me that I've put you in danger.

−It's important. She told me who the killer is.

−She did? I stood up to face her.

"Renee, who the hell is it?"

Leah entered the room and I rapidly switched back from speaking aloud to telepathic communication.

—It's okay, Leah can't hear us now.

I needed the information and I needed it *now*. She wouldn't reply. Instead, Renee fidgeted with a bracelet.

—Renee, who is it? A life is at stake. You know that, right?

—Of course I do! I'm young not stupid. Renee leaned forward in the chair and a flush of red spread across her face. *Isabella asked me to talk to Christie in person. She was worried about hot heads and emotions getting out of control. She said things had gone badly.*

—That's neither here nor there, Renee. If those two can't see sense, well, there's nothing I can do about their prejudices. But this, this is serious.

She sighed. *It's someone at work. Isabella didn't know exactly but she did say it's not Ryan. The murderer hasn't shown himself, but he has started planning.*

—I thought you knew the name of the bastard, Renee.

I gave her my best 'I can't believe you pulled that trick' look, but Renee simply glared back at me.

—Why someone at work? What's his motive?

—She didn't tell me that part because she doesn't know. Maybe you could ask her yourself.

I picked my bag up and slung it over my shoulder, breaking our connection. "I have to go. Say goodbye to your mum and dad for me. There's someone I have to see."

I made for the front door but Renee scrambled at my heels. She made a grab for my arm.

"Gyp, wait! No, don't do this, please."

Already outside, Renee reached me, breathlessly tugging at my jumper in a last ditch attempt to beg me to wait. I unlocked the car and rolled down the window.

"Renee, I get it. How could I live with myself if something happened to Christie when I know what I know? I got you involved once before. I can't do it again. I've got to go."

"She asked you to wait, that was the whole point," said Renee, grasping at the car door, which I had locked. "Wait!"

I reversed from the driveway at speed with Renee still waving at me to stop.

It wasn't going to happen. I turned the car around and made for Christie's place. I had to talk to her.

***

CHAPTER 8

Chapter Eight

Sunday 20th January, 11.22am

Christie was sitting on the side of the bed. She hadn't bothered opening the curtains. Raising her head from her lap, she saw Ryan's figure standing just inside the doorway of the darkened room. Light from the hallway cast him in silhouette. Christie sobbed.

Ryan stepped closer to her shaking figure perched on the bed. "I'm home," he said, in a quiet voice

"Oh my god," cried Christie. "I thought you were dead. I was about to call the police."

"I'm here now. Had a night out and had a few too many drinks. I'm sorry."

Christie pushed herself up from the bed and stood up on wobbly legs. "I'm sorry, I thought you were…you were…" She waited for the sobs to ease before wiping tears away. "Who were you with? Your mobile phone wasn't answering; I called you, sent messages. It's not like you, so I thought that, that—"She stepped slowly toward the kitchen, where she moved a hand to the bench for support.

"It doesn't matter who I was with. I drank too much. It was dumb. I'm sorry." Ryan took a small step away from her.

"I don't understand. Was last night really that bad?" Christie stood facing Ryan, taking in his disheveled appearance and lowered head, as if he were unable to meet her eyes.

"I don't want to talk about it, okay? I'm home."

But that wasn't all that mattered, not to her. There was something wrong, something he wasn't telling her. Was he—could he have been—with another woman? "But where were you? It's not like you to drink much."

Ryan fixed a bloodshot stare on Christie. "Well, I did, didn't I? After last night's farce, are you surprised? What a waste of time." He threw his keys, phone and wallet on the bench, where they landed with such force that they skidded off the end and clattered to the floor.

Christie thought she detected the faint scent of vomit emanating from Ryan's clothes.

"What's going on? Why won't you tell me what happened?" Christie grabbed a cloth and scrubbed at a non-existent spot on the kitchen bench.

Ryan strode toward her and spoke through clenched teeth. "What, you think I was with another woman?" His laugh was brittle. "Maybe I plan on poisoning you so I could run off with her, is that what this is?"

Christie pushed at his chest. She didn't want to tell him that the thought had crossed her mind. Now, after him staying out until 11 a.m. on a Sunday morning, she knew, just *knew* that something was going on. Why else was he reacting this way? It was completely out of character. He was *weird*. What happened to the caring, supportive Ryan? Where did he go?

"Well, where were you?"

"I can't believe you asked me that." Ryan stormed out of the room, heading for the living area at the front of the house. As Christie followed, she saw a hazy figure behind the frosted glass of the front door, where the bell chimed just seconds after registering the figure standing there.

Ryan cursed under his breath, but swung open the door. Standing there was Gypsy Shields, out of breath and shoving hair out of her eyes.

"Ryan, look, I know you probably don't want to talk–"

"What exactly is your fucking problem?"

For a moment Gypsy stood unmoving, mouth open.

"In case you didn't understand the first time, let me say it again. Fuck off and leave us alone!" He slammed the door closed so hard that the doorframe rang a second chime as it vibrated.

"Jesus, Ryan," whispered Christie.

He turned to face her. "What? Worried I might offend her? Please. Some people won't take no for an answer." He strode back down the hall. From their bedroom, she heard the slam of doors and creak of hinges.

"She's my uncle's girlfriend. What are you doing? Ryan? *Ryan.*" Christie stood at Ryan's side as he dragged a bag out of the bottom of the wardrobe. He began pulling clothing out at random and stuffing it into the duffle bag.

"Out of here. I've had enough of this shit." He moved to the drawers, which he ripped open. One of them clattered to the floor. He scrunched items up into a ball before packing them.

"What has got into you? This is crazy, completely out of control. Don't leave now, not like this." Christie reached out for him, and he batted her hand away.

"You really want to do this? Seriously, right now? What about us?"

Ryan dropped the bag on the floor. "Oh, for fuck's sake, what *about* us? After everything, you still don't trust me. You can't look me in the eye and tell me that. Do you really think I would try to kill you, for real? I'm that guy?"

Christie moved her hands away from her face. "No, Ryan, I know you wouldn't do that. I do trust you, I do."

"Bullshit, Christie, it's too late. I'm out of here."

Christie's knees buckled and she lay on the carpeted floor, listening to him rummaging around in the bathroom, knocking bottles over, until he huffed his way down the hall and the door crashed behind him.

Shoes clacked across the driveway, a remote beeped as he unlocked the car, the engine revved as he fired it up and rubber peeled.

Then deathly silence.

Maybe if she waited here long enough, the heartache would be over, death would sneak up and throw its cloak around her. Everything would stop, the heartache, the pain, the not knowing. Some things simply weren't knowable, it seemed.

And so she waited.

***

Sunday 20th January, 7.38am

Connor pulled shut the door quietly behind him, listening for the click as it locked. He didn't want to wake Gypsy. The goings-on of the day before had sapped nearly every reserve of strength he had. He looked forward to the distraction of other people's problems. Gang-related homicides and fatalities left him thankful for what he had. Carnage seemed to put things in perspective.

He had Gypsy, Christie, a satisfying career where he'd finally regained back the respect lost last year during the Aaron saga.

Connor pressed down on the security pad to enter the police building. Usually at this time of day, there were very few signs of life. On his morning run, Connor had chewed over last night's events. His mislaid belief that two of the most important women in his life, Gypsy and Christie, would find common ground and possibly form a friendship was in vain. He'd been living in a fantasyland. Time to face reality.

As Connor powered up his computer and eased into his office chair, he wondered if his intense love for both women had clouded his judgment. Since the death of her grandfather, Christie had taken to visiting her brother in jail when previously she'd written him off as a waste of space, an aberration of the family gene pool. She'd begun mentioning him in conversation, and had shown a greater interest in her nephew Bailey, who was under the watchful eye of his ex-wife Jill. He'd even discovered she'd taken to babysitting him, not like her at all. Children were to her an afterthought, something for her to think about in later years. Christie had always enjoyed her freedom and independence, and he wondered what was going on in that head of hers.

Connor had moved on. He hadn't the slightest urge to visit his nephew.

Of course, he of all people knew what grief could do to someone—alter their perception, change the way they viewed the world, and shift alliances. He'd seen it happen with Aaron. He'd be damned if it would happen to Christie.

He logged in and opened his emails, and noticed one from head office advising the team that Ryan Martin would not be in; he'd taken the day off sick.

Retrieving his mobile phone from the jacket thrown over the back of his chair, he dialed the number, bringing it to his ear but there was no answer. Instead, he sent a text message. *Hope all is well mate. Give me a call when you can.* Best to keep it low key and casual.

What struck him was that Gypsy had known that Christie's hair was falling out. Not that he doubted Gypsy—hell, he'd struggled with his own abilities enough times to know where she was coming from. He had no idea why it was called a 'gift.' More like a curse if anything. He'd let his sentinel abilities lay dormant. Using them would open the door to drama and danger, and he went through enough danger at work. He certainly didn't need anything extra in that department. He knew Gypsy well enough to know that she would follow the vision to determine its ultimate meaning, even if it disturbed Christie and Ryan and made them uncomfortable. Hell, if he admitted it fully, the wriggle of discomfort crept up on him at times, despite being a sentinel. Both secrets would leave him too exposed, and if there was one thing, he'd learned in the police force, chinks in the armor were best kept close to one's chest.

He could lose Christie, his only niece, probably his only child. With Aaron locked up, his brother and sister-in-law dead, he wasn't prepared to jeopardize his relationship with Christie. Gypsy would need to let this one go, and if anyone could convince her of that, he could.

As he picked up the investigation book to go over a recent homicide, he toyed with the idea of getting in touch with this Isabella character again. A night with Gypsy at home would do both of them the world of good. He'd check in with Christie on Monday when the dust had settled, maybe take her out to lunch.

***

Sunday 20th January, 1.54pm

I took a step down from Ryan and Christie's front porch, limbs like jelly.

What just happened? I knew they were pissed off, but seriously. This was something more, beyond what had happened Saturday night. Ryan's door slamming fury seemed out of character. For the year I'd known him, he'd been a caring, at times abrupt but ultimately supportive boyfriend in Christie's background. His reaction was weird. I'd felt sure Ryan held secrets close to his chest. His reaction had been too extreme.

Since the loss of Christie's grandfather, Ryan seemed to be a supportive partner to Christie and his usual impatience had faded away into insignificance. Obviously, it was back with a vengeance. How had he morphed into a raging hothead slamming doors in my face? It didn't make any sense.

There was something he wouldn't tell anyone, and I would be the one to find out.

Summoning up my determination, setting my shoulders and fixing my gaze on the interior of my parked vehicle, I unlocked my car and started it up. I drove to a safer location a couple of streets away, where I could speak to Connor in peace without being concerned that Ryan might turn green and bust open his shirt with muscles bulging, and storm over to smash the windows to rage at me.

Surprisingly, although he was at work, Connor answered my call at once. "Gypsy, what's up?"

"I'm just outside Ryan and Christie's place."

"Oh, god." There was a silence of a few seconds that seemed to go on forever.

"Look, I wouldn't have gone over there, but I saw Renee today and Isabella has visited her, too."

"Shit. I wish you hadn't done that, it's still too raw after last night. I thought that's what we agreed on. What happened?"

"I didn't get a chance to talk to either of them. I said no more than a few words. Ryan was screaming at Christie. I heard him through the door—which he slammed in my face after hurling abuse my way, too. I'm still shaking."

Another steely silence. Then, "Gypsy, don't go over there again without me. Next time–"

"Connor, there might not be a bloody next time! Isabella knows who it is."

"What? Who?"

"It's someone Christie works with. Ryan seems to think I pointed the finger at him, which I didn't. I only told her what Isabella told me."

"I know that."

"So what do we do? Can we go over there together?"

"Leave it with me. I need to work out the best approach."

"Fucking hell, Connor, tomorrow is Monday. Christie's back at work then and we both know she's walking into a death trap."

"I have to go, I'm sorry. We'll talk tonight. Don't do anything more until I see you, okay?"

I sighed. "Yeah, okay, Connor."

I started the car up and got moving. Connor definitely had a soft spot when it came to Christie, but then she was possibly his only child. He and Jill, his ex-wife, had tried to have children, navigating the maze of IVF, but no dice.

Tonight I had to get through to him. We had to visit Christie. Even if she and Ryan refused to budge, we had to do something. Maybe we could leave a note under the door. An easy way out to appease Connor but it might save her life. If anything happened to Christie, I knew my conscience would destroy me, and I'd become my own executioner. There was no way I'd be going down that road, no matter how much I loved Connor.

***

Sunday 20th January, 8.14pm

After dinner, I lolled around on the couch with a book. I read the same page at least four times, casting glances at Connor, who remained silent as a stone. He watched a movie, staring at the screen with a blank face. I knew from experience that when turmoil hit, he'd clam up and shut down. A storm brewed.

It was his way of punishing me and it drove me crazy. Sure, the man was hot, and amazing in so many ways, but giving me the silent treatment was infuriating. The time had come for him to knock it off.

As the credits rolled, I decided I'd go to bed, even if I went to bed without him. I stood up and considered Connor. He'd rolled the full length of his limbs out on the floor, resting his head on a cushion.

"I'm going to bed. Coming?" I had to get one parting shot before I called it a night. He didn't show that he'd heard my question. Either he'd succumbed to tiredness or something else brewed. I knew he was involved in an intense investigation at work. Maybe the sulking meant he could switch off from the serial assault case he'd mentioned briefly, or he wanted to punish me for forcing him to face his paternity issues. It didn't make sense—he'd seemed fine earlier.

"Come on. We need to see what Isabella has to say. Tomorrow's the big day."

He murmured something, but with his chin tucked into his neck, I couldn't make it out.

"What?"

"I'll sleep here, on the couch."

"What the hell? When did you get so moody? What's going on?"

He sighed and pulled his frame up from the floor to lie across the couch. He settled there with one hand propping up his head.

He mumbled, staring at the floor, "I'm not sure about this Isabella business. There's no accountability, no proof. She could be some random dead kid playing mind games. Where does that leave us with Ryan and Christie?"

"You mean, where does that leave *you* with Ryan and Christie. I don't believe this. You've done a 180-degree turn in a couple of hours. What gives?"

"If Christie is my daughter, where does that leave me—leave us? She can't stand the sight of either one of us. Because what? Because some ghost told us she's going to be poisoned? What if Christie isn't in danger? I lose my niece—possibly my daughter—forever. I don't know if she'll ever forgive me for meddling. I had to talk her and Ryan into the reading and when it did happen, it was a damn disaster. She still doesn't trust you."

"Of course she doesn't, but that says more about her than me."

His eyebrows flicked upward.

"Seriously, Connor, how do you know she's not in danger? She certainly doesn't, and won't accept it. I'm not willing to chance it, are you? So she hates me for a bit. Big deal—she'll live!"

"She's all I have left."

"Oh, for fuck's sake, Connor! What the hell am I, then?" He'd wimped out. *Fucking hell.*

I sighed and uncrossed my arms, letting them drop to my sides. "At least one of us has to stick their neck out here. I thought it would be both of us, but I guess it's just me. I always knew you as a man of integrity, Connor. I'm not so sure tonight."

I couldn't believe this. At the time it had hit the fan, all had been well, my relief palpable. Suddenly now, after the fact, he'd decided we weren't on the same team anymore. What had got into him?

"You're telling me you've changed that quickly? I don't believe it for a fucking minute."

Connor pushed himself up and approached me with dark eyes. I backed toward the kitchen bench. He grabbed me around the waist.

While I loved the man, his unpredictability at present was my undoing. He'd always been so supportive, even tempered, my stable rock amongst a sea of chaos. Right now, my rock had crumbled.

Not only was I overwhelmed, he was really starting to piss me off.

"What's up with you? You're bouncing from one moment to the next what–"

Then he kissed me and his lips crushed mine. His kiss, usually tender, was firm and demanding. Taken aback, I placed my arms on his chest and made a muffled noise, which gradually faded away.

Despite myself, my body flooded with warmth and I returned his kiss.

Connor and I had never made love when angry. This was a first. What was going through his head? Staking his claim? That wasn't like the man I fell in love with at all. This was *weird* but as he'd clammed shut, I didn't plan on getting an explanation.

He cupped my buttocks with his hands, lifting me up and onto the bench.

I opened my mouth and Connor's tongue began probing, searching, as his hands pushed up my skirt. I threw my arms around his back and he pushed me back onto the bench.

As he pushed himself against me, I felt that Connor was erect. My skirt was pushed up to my waist, and the next moment his lips, his tongue, his teeth were on my neck. I trembled with desire, warmth surging through my chest. Yet as Connor reached up to remove my underwear, I paused.

I attempted to push him away yet again, firmer this time. Connor was my object of desire—hell I had a sneaking suspicion he was the object of other women's desires too, he was gorgeous to look at—but did I want to be with him like this?

Did I really want this, regardless of the situation? Did Connor?

As Connor pulled away to gaze at me with hooded eyes, his lips swollen and wet, I realized I didn't want to be part of Connor's fury, an outlet, a release. Even though my heart thudded in my chest and my body cried out for him. Not now.

"No, Connor. Not like this," I said.

"What?" he said. His lips were engorged, and his face flushed. He brought his head back down to my neck. "I know you love me. You want this too…"

My hands moved to his chest, and I pushed him, lightly at first. Connor took a step away from me. His breathing sounded ragged, and he ran his fingers through his hair.

"I thought…," he mumbled.

I stood pulling at my skirt and rearranging my clothing. "I can't resist you, you know that. Not like this, though. It's not—" I let the remainder of the sentence hang in mid-air, gathering my thoughts.

A muscle twitched in Connor's cheek and he moved toward me again. "You won't know until you try it," he whispered and began kissing my neck again, and a shiver ran down my spine.

"No," I said, and nudged his shoulders, increasing the space between us. I couldn't meet his gaze.

"Not like this. I'm sorry, I just can't." Adjusting my clothing, I headed for the stairs. I placed one hand on the railing and turned to him. "I hope you understand."

Connor shook his head.

"Are you coming to bed?"

"No," he said and disappeared, presumably to find bedding to sleep on the couch. I made my way up the stairs and undressed before sliding under the covers.

In the year, Connor and I had been together, this had never happened. I understood his fear of having the talk with Christie. What I didn't understand was how he seemed to be responding to it. Of all the times to make love, why now?

I tossed and turned in bed, wondering what caused Connor's mood. I wondered if he was attempting to mend bridges. If so, this wasn't the way to do it, surely he knew that. If he was trying to distract me from the Christie issue, he didn't have a chance in hell.

CHAPTER 9

Monday 21st January, 2.38am

The glow from the computer screen lit up the figure hunched over the desk in the corner of the lounge room. Brenton had tried to go back to sleep, but thoughts rolled around in his head, one leading to the next and to the next until the room began spinning. Time to get up and work out how he could put his master plan into action. This would need a thoroughly mapped course with every eventuality considered.

Of course, he loved Christie, there was no question of that, but he loved Ryan more. He had to have him, every inch of him, every thought, and every part of his life. Of course, Ryan protested that he wasn't that way inclined. Of course he would, it was to be expected. He'd convinced himself that Christie was the only one for him, but Brenton knew that anyone could convince themselves of anything given the right circumstances. All they usually needed was a gentle push in the right direction to shake their convictions off.

Once Ryan was torn up by the grief of Christie in hospital, he'd need comfort, support, guidance, someone to pick up the pieces, and Brenton was the man to do it. Ryan would fall into his arms. He'd have nowhere else to fall.

Brenton had done his research, and the easiest way would be to slip something into her morning coffee. After nearly an hour of searching, he smiled as he found what he was looking for. It was traceless, colorless, and odorless. It had a sweet taste, and could be used in place of sugar. Medical tests would not uncover it, unless hospital staff specifically looked for it, which of course they wouldn't, considering at first Christie would appear drunk, followed by a seemingly miraculous recovery a day later. However, by the second day, her internal organs would go into failure, one by one, while Christie appeared to all intents and purposes to be recovering nicely. Hyperventilation, shortness of breath, followed by heart failure would leave hospital staff frantically searching for an undiscovered genetic heart defect, and nothing would be found.

By the third day, Christie would suffer kidney failure. Brenton figured this gave him three days to decide when to make the call and inform the hospital staff (anonymously, of course) of what to look for. He wasn't convinced of her death, he loved her, just a scare to help Ryan see what was truly important—Brenton had a great deal of affection for the woman; she'd just been born highly strung, is all. Besides, by the third day, he and Ryan would be a long way away from Melbourne, far enough that they could never be traced.

Brenton left his office chair and headed to the garage. He flicked the outdoor light on and, grabbing the step rail, clomped down three concrete steps to the small garage.

The sensor flicked the lights on as he entered. The smell of encrusted dust, which had settled onto the light fittings and shelves, reached his nose. Weaving past the lawn mower, his small, rarely driven car and a long forgotten bicycle, Brenton found what he was looking for.

Perfect. That should do it. He poured a cupful into a plastic bottle and sealed it tightly before tucking it under his arm.

He made his way back up the stairs, humming quietly to himself.

He left the bottle inside a bag, which he would take with him in the morning. Brenton dropped his shoulders.

Events would occur effortlessly; it was a faultless plan, the perfect solution, a way out. Turning back the covers, Brenton sighed and got into bed. He turned off the small glass lamp on the matching antique side table and closed his eyes. In a minute or so, with deep breaths, Brenton relaxed for the first in a long time and slept like a baby.

***

Monday 20th January, 3.27am

I wrestled with sleep for what felt like the entire night, but realistically was more likely a couple of hours. My insomnia didn't give in that easily. There she stood at the bottom of the bed, waiting patiently for my attention, hanging around the corner of my bed.

—Gypsy, wake up.

—What do you mean, wake up? I'm asleep, I'm dreaming.

—I know who he is. He's shown himself.

—Leave me alone.

—Someone's grumpy.

—I hope you're right, Isabella. So far, Christie and Ryan believe I'm the devil incarnate and the man I love has chickened out. There's quite a bit at stake. I could lose everything here.

I sighed, realizing I'd snapped at a child, a spirit child but nonetheless undeserving of my grumpiness. What was *wrong* with me?

Although devastated by Connor's lack of loyalty, there was still no excuse. However, Isabella replied before I could explain.

—Like your life, you mean?

—Well, no, not like my life, but losing Connor sure comes close.

Much as I didn't like to admit it, if Connor ever left me, I'd be devastated. Isabella wasn't letting up however.

—His name is Brenton. He's close to Christie, he works with her—another graphic designer. He's helped her through the pain of losing her grandfather. But he wants her out of the way now. He's planning to poison her in the morning, leaving something in her coffee.

—Huh? Why would he want her out of the way?

—He's in love with Ryan.

I gasped, a hand coming up to my mouth.

—What? With Ryan? How did Ryan and Brenton meet?

—Yes, Brenton prefers men to women. The night you, Ryan and Christie did the reading, Ryan sped off and left Christie by the side of the road. He drank, a lot, and ended up at Brenton's favorite bar. Brenton recognized Ryan and took him home.

Not sure how to respond to that, I paused. *—But, but, what does this mean?*

—Ryan stayed the night. He woke in Brenton's bed and of course assumed the worst—but nothing happened, he was so drunk he wasn't capable of anything. Ryan doesn't know that, of course.

—Isabella, this is ridiculous. I mean, what are the odds of Ryan running into Brenton?

—If I didn't know better, I'd say Brenton planned it. I don't see how Brenton could have set it up. He believes it was the hand of fate and they were destined to be together. He hasn't had contact with Ryan before that night, but he's heard all about him from Christie. Ryan's all she can talk about.

—Fucking hell, you have to be kidding me. If they wrote me off as a nut before, they'll have me locked up in the loony bin after I tell them this. Jesus Christ.

I folded my arms across my chest. *—This is heavy, Isabella. I don't know if I can do this.*

—You can, you're stronger than you think. Besides you're already in deep, what's the harm in wading in a little bit further?

—I lose Connor. Not like this, I don't want to force him to choose between family and me again. The first time was bad enough. After my interference in the Reardon family, they take most things I say with a grain of salt now.

—Well, if he loves you the way you think he does, then none of this will matter, will it? He'll stand by you.

If I thought life tested me before now, the biggest test loomed ahead. *—What do you suggest?*

—You need to let Ryan and Christie know that it's Brenton. That he'll slip something into one of her drinks in the morning. He wants Ryan all to himself.

—Maybe. How is he doing it? What's his poison?

—He's gone to the garage. He took down a bottle of—

Shit! The connection broke with a twig-like snap. What just happened? Someone had cut the telepathic contact.

Connor. You bastard.

The only person that could cut a connection between two psychics or telepaths would be a shield, a protector, *a fucking sentinel.*

Connor, the coward, had cut us off. He wanted to end this. Well, I wouldn't go down without a fight.

My eyes snapped open and I shoved back the covers. I stormed toward the lounge room, where he flopped across the couch, seemingly asleep.

I knew better.

"Connor, wake up."

"Huh?" His shoulders rose, hair tousled, eyes marred by sleep.

"You fucking bastard! You cut us off! Of all the slimy, covert tricks, this one is good, really good. I didn't think you were capable of something like it, but obviously I underestimated you."

Connor jumped up from the couch in an instant, the veil of pretended sleep falling from him.

"The connection with Isabella just snapped mid-sentence. She's already told me who the murderer is—it's not Ryan, it's some weasel Christie works with, *Brenton* of all names. You broke the connection before she could tell me the name of the poison. You fucking *prick*!" I ripped the blanket off the couch, pounding it into a ball.

Connor brought an arm out. "Gypsy, calm down! What are you going on about? Listen–"

"I'm not listening to you again! The only person capable of cutting off my talk with Isabella would be someone who can block psychic signals, a protector, and a guard. You know, like a fucking sentinel. Know any of those?" The blood raged through me, every nerve, every hair on high alert.

"Gypsy, it's not like that. Of course I want to save Christie's life, I love her."

"Really, so what happens if she turns up poisoned tomorrow and ends up in a hospital? What do we tell the doctors to search for, huh? Ryan and Christie already think I'm a complete fucking idiot, and by the sound of it so do you! Christ, Connor, of all people I thought you'd understand." I stamped to the kitchen, planning to make a hot drink. How I'd get back to sleep now I had no idea.

"Connor, don't insult my intelligence and tell me you don't know what I'm talking about, *please*."

He gazed at me with round eyes, the blanket at his feet where I'd thrown it.

"I just want this to stop, Gypsy. I've already lost my brother, my ex-wife, my nephew. All I have left is Christie. I'm not losing her, too."

"But don't you get it? If we don't stop this prick Brenton, you'll lose her for good! You're not making any sense!"

I couldn't believe this. He'd never cut a telepathic connection before, ever, but then again I'd never given him the chance. He had it all fully justified in his own head, even though he could be putting Christie in danger. I'd drink my hot chocolate and stumble back to bed.

Maybe if I could get back to sleep, I could establish the connection with Isabella afresh. I only needed a few seconds to get the name of the poison.

I poured the warm water into a mug and stirred in my hot chocolate, picked up the cup and left the kitchen. Connor sat on the couch with the blanket around his shoulders, staring at the flickering pictures on the TV with the volume down.

"I'm going back to bed," I said. "One of us needs to try and salvage the situation and save your daughter's arse."

He didn't glare back.

***

Monday 21ˢᵗ January, 9.55am

I awoke the next morning to light streaming between the closed curtains and my telephone ringing off the hook. I rolled over to my left to contemplate the electronic green figures on the alarm clock.

Shit, I'd slept in! The clock blared at me, 9.55 a.m. The alarm usually woke me around 7.30 a.m. I'd left my mobile phone downstairs, and could hear the ringtone pinging relentlessly. After a two second pause, it began again. Someone *really* wanted to talk to me. Throwing back the covers and swiping the hair from my eyes, I began the trek downwards. Swinging open the door to my study, I searched for the source of the noise. My phone in its purple case lay open on my desk, buzzing furiously almost falling off the desk.

I picked it up and saw the name on the screen. I swiped it and held it to my ear.

"Connor," I panted, out of breath from the race downstairs.

"Gypsy? I called a few times, you worried me."

"Sorry, I can't believe I slept in. My alarm didn't go off. What's going on?"

"Christie's in hospital." His deep voice gave little away.

Holy crap, it had happened.

"Oh my god, when?"

"Not long ago, Ryan called. She's at St Vincent's now; I'm on my way there."

"What's wrong with her?"

"She collapsed at work. She said she felt sick, nauseous. She threw up in the ambulance, but now she's making no sense, hallucinating."

"I'll meet you there, out the front."

"Yes, she'll probably still be in emergency. Call me when you get there."

I hung up and dropped the phone on my desk. My hands were shaking and my heart banged like a shed door in the wind.

Oh my god. I'd hoped Isabella and I were overreacting, but now it had happened. We were right. At that moment, I never thought I'd say it, but I wanted to be wrong, the wrongest I'd ever been.

My mouth flew open and I shuffled back a step.

I stamped upstairs, sprinting into my bedroom, racing back and forth to find clothes closest to me, and cleanest. Pulling my hair back into a ponytail, I jumped down the stairs, grabbed my bag and keys from the kitchen and headed for the car.

In the twenty minutes it took me to get to the hospital, I ran through scenarios in my head, all of which went nowhere without a solution. I was right; the professionals could take it from here. Isabella had led me in the right direction, even if Ryan insisted on my lunacy and Connor sat on the fence.

I needed Isabella.

Power walking from the car park to the hospital's front entrance, I called Connor.

"Gypsy, where are you?"

"Out the front of the hospital."

"Come around and see us. We're in the Banksia unit around the back."

"Okay, see you in a sec." I hung up and recommenced panting as I strode around the building toward the rear of the complex.

Unfortunately, I knew what admission to the Banksia unit meant. Christie had been placed in a psychiatric ward. *Good god what next?*

Puffing my way to the edge of the complex, I spied the sign and headed through the sliding doors, the main entrance to the unit. There Connor sat, his long legs stretched to full length. He seemed huge on the tiny cheap visitor's chairs. When he saw me, he jerked his body up and out of its perch in the plastic chair and bounded toward me.

"Connor!"

"Gypsy, glad you came."

"How could I not? How is she?"

"Come with me." Connor loped along the corridor and I followed his lead.

"She vomited repeatedly, and slurred her speech like she'd been drinking. Now she's hallucinating, spouting the weirdest things. Talking about slimy creatures climbing through the windows to come and attack her. Ryan spoke to the staff about the stress she's been under, losing her grandfather and her hair falling out, although I'm not sure that in the face of her babbling she should be in the Banksia unit. I guess that's Ryan's call to argue the point."

"My god, Connor she isn't mad, it's the poison!"

"We don't have any proof of that."

"Yet."

"Let's just play it by ear for now. Conflict isn't going to help anyone."

"Since when did you get to sit on the fence? You're a sentinel; you've been in contact with Isabella, how can you deny this is real, and that Christie really has been poisoned?"

He paused before a closed beige door at the end of the carpeted corridor. "I want to hold onto what I've got."

"Does that include me?"

"Look, let's keep this low key for now, okay? We're in a psychiatric ward." Connor had dropped his voice to hushed tones, and as he pushed down on the door handle, a nurse seated at a desk shot me a wan smile. Connor ushered me through the corridor and a dark, longhaired man with a haunted, vacant expression grunted at me.

"It's okay, she's in here," whispered Connor.

We turned into a small, brightly lit room and there slumped Christie in a plastic chair of a different color. She hunched over a kidney dish.

Seeing her like this threw me. I glanced at Connor. While we hadn't got along, I would never have wished this on her, not in the slightest.

Ryan hovered at her side, his face creased and worn.

"Connor," he whispered, extending his hand to shake hands.

"Ryan. I came as soon as I heard."

Ryan shifted his gaze to me briefly. "You brought her with you." He obviously couldn't acknowledge me yet. If I didn't know better, his frayed temper would have puzzled me, considering his reputation as Christie's staunchest supporter and provider of support and care. Now I knew better thanks to Isabella. A one-night stand with a man could do that to a straight guy's conscience. Cheating was cheating whether with the same sex or the opposite, as far as I knew, in fact as far as most people knew.

"How is she?" Both of their eyes turned to Christie, whose hair hung across her face.

"Uncle Connor," she said through dry, cracked lips.

Connor moved quickly to squat beside her. "Christie, honey, I'm here."

"Beedlejenkblarncraum. There, over there!" She screeched and pointed to the window.

"It's okay, Christie," he murmured, "I'll get them. They'll never hurt you."

Could have fooled me.

With a crack of the knees, Connor stood up.

"Maybe we should take this out to the corridor." He stepped toward me and gestured toward the doorway.

Ryan leaned closer to Christie, murmuring soothing words and smoothing down her hair. "I'll be out in a sec," said Ryan, turning his head toward us before moving his attention back to Christie.

In a split second, Christie bolted upright and scooted in my direction. She waved her arms manically, eyes bulging, the pallor of her colorless face highlighted in the morning sun.

"You bitch–fucking thing! Brother, my flesh, bleeding burning brother. Hurt him, trapped and tortured, crucified, vicious nasty hag, old witch…"

Shit. I knew exactly what she meant, and I wondered if Ryan did. This outburst certainly confirmed a few things. Someone *had* been visiting the scumbag in jail.

Ryan turned back to Christie to murmur what I could only assume were soothing words in an effort to placate her, and I quickened my steps to reach Connor in the corridor.

The top of my head reached Connor's chin, and he bent slightly to whisper in my ear.

"I'm not sure if this is a good idea. You being here might have set her off."

"If so, that would be because a cobra is whispering in her ear. She's easily led."

"He's her brother, Gypsy!"

"Yeah, and your nephew, who just happens to be cooling his heels in jail since he shot a cop. Blood isn't always thicker than water, is it?"

As Connor turned his gaze elsewhere, I saw a muscle in his cheek flicker. He didn't want to say it. Yet it didn't matter whether he said it aloud or not, I knew him inside out, knew every inch of him, warts and all. I had a fair idea what he was thinking.

"That's different."

"Really, how? Because he chose to be a victim, to slide down a spiral of hate and anger. That was his choice, not yours. As you said, he was never going to change, no matter what. I know Christie's your last and closest blood relative, but regardless of how you feel about this, blood tests need to be done, and fast. If you love her like you say you do, have the damn test. I want to save her, not punish her. I thought you of all people knew that."

His eyes met mine. I scrutinized his face. I recognized the flush, the dark eyes, and the clenched fist. A tidal wave of emotion swam beneath the surface, but of course, Connor would never let on. Ryan appeared, standing between us.

He pushed out a breath and rubbed his brow. "She's calmed down, for now, anyway. What the hell is with the weird arse torture story?"

So Christie hadn't told him. My focus didn't move from Connor's face. "Ancient history."

"It should never have come to this. I should have known. The stress, the grief, it's overwhelmed her. She needs rest." Ryan shook his head.

Damn right, it should never have come to this.

"She needs a blood test is what she needs. Did you ask the medical staff to check for poisoning?" I directed my question to Connor rather than Ryan.

A heavy cloud passed across Ryan's face. "Believe it or not, I did, against my better judgment. They took blood as soon as she got here."

Connor, as usual, played the mediator, the soother of frayed nerves. "Some rest will do her good."

"If they don't know what the poison is, how the hell will they look for it? Meanwhile she's the victim of another poison—whatever psychiatric med they decide on in their endless wisdom." I struggled to keep the sarcasm out of my voice, and of course, failed miserably. I had my own experience with psychiatrists in years gone by, and wouldn't spit on them if their collective arses were on fire. They ruined lives, and I'd be damned if I'd let them ruin Christie's.

Ryan's feet were planted wide, and he gestured at my chest with a pointed finger. "Listen; mind your own fucking business. We never asked you–"

"Actually, you did." My tone had flat lined with the last of my sympathy depleted. Playing nice for

Connor's sake didn't sit well with me anymore. Time to lay out some cold hard truths. "I'm a messenger, nothing more nothing less. I don't make this shit up to play mind games, and at no point did I make any accusations. The two of you dubbed that in."

"You cheeky fucking–" Ryan would probably explode at any second—his cheeks puffed out and face changing color—but I'd started and meant to finish.

I took a step forward and pointed right back at him. "No, you're the only one here with the hide to accuse me of god knows what. You have the wrong fucking target and I'm tired of it, completely *over* it! I've wondered for a while now why you're acting so goddam out of character. Then it all made sense, once Isabella pointed me in the right direction."

"It's time for you to leave," he said, the snarl in his voice increasing in volume.

"Really? You don't want to hear who's poisoning your girl. Newsflash, it's not you—but if I were making shit up as I went along, surely I'd point the finger at you? You've given me every reason to, but you're not that evil. You just can't take your fucking blinkers off."

Ryan turned his back to me and swore under his breath. Connor attempted to get my attention.

"Gypsy—" The warning tone in his voice struck me like a stop sign, a red light, but there remained little chance of stopping me now.

"It's a work colleague, a fellow graphic designer. They've become best friends, and Christie's told him all about you. He believes he knows you already, and I think the two of you have already crossed paths, right? You and Brenton? Who else would have the motive to sweep Christie out of the way? Then he'd have you all to himself." I leaned back and crossed my arms, waiting for the fuse to ignite.

"You stupid fucking bitch," he spat through clenched teeth. He lunged for me, and Connor sharply stepped between us, staring Ryan down. Ryan turned to the wall, where a set of orange plastic chairs were stacked, and grappled with one of them, tearing them apart with a crash, flinging one of them down the corridor.

It skidded along for a few meters, coming to a stop two rooms down with its legs in the air like a defeated insect.

Some of the patients emerged from doorways, eyes wide and wet hands in mouths. The man with the long, dark hair and cavernous eyes giggled.

From the end of the corridor a nurse and a burly security guard headed our way, their arms pistons and mouths set in lines of grim determination.

"Excuse me," said the security guard "I'm afraid we're going to have to ask you to leave the premises."

"It's her, the bitch is goading me, chuck her out!"

Connor grasped Ryan's forearm, restraining him. "Let's not make this any worse than it already is."

With blank, unseeing eyes, Ryan traipsed beside Connor, appearing chastised by Connor's take-charge tone, head down, his sudden obedience casting some sense of calm at last.

Connor stopped before the two rather stern figures. "I'm so sorry, I do apologize, we'll go outside to cool off."

"We simply can't tolerate violence of any kind. Please ask your friends to calm down and remain composed when they return."

Connor nodded. "I'll see that they do."

We treaded toward the main entrance silently. As we reached the doors, they swished open and a light breeze waved us out.

"I think some food, rest and new perspective will do both of you the world of good," lectured Connor, his expression grim.

"Okay," I said.

"I'll check in with you later. Message me if there's any change." Connor nodded before conferring with Ryan, who had lit up a cigarette. At something Connor said, he jerked his head in the semblance of a nod.

I marched back to my car, eager to get the hell out of there and back to the safety of my small but familiar flat.

CHAPTER 10

Chapter Ten

Monday 21st January, 6.17pm

Jake couldn't shake the creeping along his skin, or the voice in the back of his mind whispering hoarsely that he knew what he was like; Brenton would do something stupid.

He knew that Brenton liked to blab to friends that they'd broken up because of his 'baggage,' and he hadn't bothered correcting them. It would set off Brenton's inbuilt drama alert and that only led to a scene, usually a nasty one.

He liked Brenton, and they'd comforted each other with companionship and sex for quite a few months. There didn't seem to be any harm in it—a good time had been had by all and they'd discussed the nature of the relationship up front like the two mature adults they were, or so he thought. He'd later realized that Brenton had oh-so-conveniently blocked that conversation from his memory and flicked on the white noise switch when they'd agreed to take time to determine compatibility before committing to monogamy. It had been an easygoing friendship there for a while, and it had been good for the briefest of periods.

Until the night Jake, left Roberto's with a friend, without Brenton.

He remembered the night so vividly. They were parked outside his place. The streetlight shone across the dash of the car as, with knees turned to each other, they chatted easily, moving from one subject to the next with ease. Jake enjoyed being around someone so handsome and mature, plus he had a brain. He was almost intellectual, in fact. The smooth conversation flowed and Jake enjoyed the deep timbre voice of Cam, a straight-acting insurance actuary who made a lot of sense. Jake anticipated lounging in the living area with a glass of wine, seeing where the conversation would take them and if it would lead to anything further as both of them felt their way around the heavily veiled conversation, assessing and measuring, wondering if the spark would be enough to carry them any further.

The car behind them lurched forward and a loud crunch put an end to any conversation at all. A figure jumped from the offending car. Jake swung the door open and turned to the source of the smash.

"What the hell?" Jake demanded as he reached the tree at the side of his home. The streetlight caught the offender's face, revealing a familiar jawline. "Brenton? Are you fucking mental?"

"You've got a nerve accusing me, you—you—*Judas*. How could you betray me like this?"

"Betray you? What are you on?"

"Who the hell is that?" Brenton gestured at Cam. Cameron had his hands in his pockets, and took a step toward Jake.

"I'll be on my way. I'll catch a cab."

"Don't do that, Cam. I'm so sorry, this is crazy. Let me drive you home."

"It's okay, mate, I'm out of here. See you at the club sometime." He turned away from them both, storming toward the nearest main road.

Jake's voice gurgled in the back of his throat. "What the fucking hell is wrong with you?"

"You, that's what. You treat me like shit, you think it's okay to take anyone home with you?"

"You act like I do this all the time—and that's apart from the fact that it's none of your business what I do in the privacy of my own home, or outside it. We agreed, we discussed this, remember?"

"How convenient."

Jake rubbed his forehead before coming to a decision and folding his arms. "This is it. We're done, Brent. Complete bullshit. You're lucky I didn't hurt you. What the fuck are you going to do about my car?

"It's only a car. What about my feelings?"

Jake wanted to hurt Brenton, make him see sense. He knew that would only make things worse, so he took a moment to regain some self-control.

Jake took a step away from him before spinning back to point a finger at Brenton's eyes.

"You are deluded. You will fix my car, or I fix you."

"Very childish."

"Hilarious coming from you, Brent. Now piss off and go home before I do what my fists were made to do and break your nose."

"That'd be right, typical Neanderthal response."

"It's a damn sight better than smashing my car for no reason other than petty, unjustified jealousy."

"Fine, I'm going home then. Your loss."

To add insult to injury, Brenton fluffed around the car before getting in, making sure of its condition. He examined the front end, then frowned and glared at Jake.

"You broke my light."

Jake grabbed Brenton and shoved him onto the front of the car, pushing the back of his skull so that one side of his face pressed firmly against the bonnet. He grappled him, jerking his arm up behind his back so hard that Brenton squealed.

"Ouch, you're hurting me, stop!"

Jake leaned in close, so that his lips moved inches from Brenton's ear.

"Listen here, you neurotic, deluded prick. We agreed we wouldn't be exclusive. Now you smash up my car while I'm talking to the one person who seems half-decent. Tell me why I shouldn't break your arm?"

"Because we're friends." Brenton whimpered and began to cry.

Bloody hell.

Jake exhaled, and pushed Brenton up and away from the car before releasing his hold. He almost felt sorry for the guy. Obviously lonely and completed screwed up, he needed help.

Brenton turned to glare at Jake, eyes wide, before scrambling into the car.

As Brenton took off, Jake ran his fingers through his hair and blew out a breath.

So why did Jake follow Brenton here, where he'd decided to set up camp outside Ryan's house? Why now, after all this time and all he had been through?

Because Brenton needed a friend and, unfortunately, Jake knew he figured prominently as one of the few people that knew him inside and out and accepted Brenton for the person he really was. Jake had resigned himself to being the only decent friend the guy had.

He peered into the rear vision mirror. There Brenton sat, just as expected. Stalking a police officer that wanted nothing to do with him.

Jake got out of the car, arms hanging by his side, and waited while Brenton unlocked his driver's side door.

The negotiations began in earnest.

***

Monday 21*st* January, 7.02pm

As I rolled my car into the driveway, I yanked on the hand brake, which screamed in protest. Of all the nerve.

I'd been patient, loyal and done my best to accommodate Connor's resentful daughter. The daughter he couldn't bring himself to acknowledge as a product of the affair with his sister-in-law. No more.

He'd made his choice, and now I'd made mine. If he cringed at having the conversation with Christie, I'd just have to step up and take it on.

I unlocked the door and the smell of slowly decaying food greeted me.

Great. I'd have to do some housework.

I climbed the stairs to my room and threw on my last clean tracksuit. Stepping back downstairs, I pounded the stereo until the sounds of the local radio station rose. Then I yanked open the cupboard door, knocking over cleaning materials until I found what I needed. Time for some therapeutic furious cleaning to clear the decks.

As I cleared the benches prior to scrubbing them down, I wondered if I'd exhaust myself to the point where I'd actually sleep for a change. I damn well hoped so. Isabella owed me some answers and I wouldn't take no for an answer.

***

Monday 21st January, 7.39pm

Connor sat beside Christie, who had thankfully packed herself back into bed. She didn't look good—a gray pallor was spreading across her skin, and a lock of hair hung over her face. It blew upwards as she let out a breath.

He wondered what she thought, what went through that head of hers. Had the hallucinations taken hold?

The niece he knew in all likelihood deserved acknowledgement as his daughter. She had become so precious to him over the years, but he couldn't say it aloud. Would he lose her to the grips of insanity, as she spun out of control in a world of her own making until she lost every grip on reality?

Thinking about it wouldn't help. When she recovered, he'd suggest an outing, something special. Maybe the beach or a picnic in the botanical gardens. As each minute passed, the knowledge that she could slip away from him, sinking into oblivion without ever knowing how much she truly meant to him, burned at Connor, almost choking him.

He wouldn't lose her, he couldn't. Connor kicked off his shoes and pushed his back into the chair, stretching out and making himself as comfortable as possible in a hard backed hospital chair. A night guarding his daughter would be a karmic release, a penance for not spending more time with her, for ignoring his duty and failing to confront the most difficult conversation he might ever have. It seemed the current crisis had forced the issue.

Please, if she recovered from this, he would make it up to her, be the father that she needed.

He just hoped he'd get the chance to tell her what she meant to him.

***

Monday 21st January, 8.36pm

Ryan arrived home and as the engine purred, his dull eyes fixed on an acacia bush. Flicking the ignition off, he opened the car and got out, the ache of exhaustion burning its way through his legs, and he massaged his temple as the dull ache of a headache took hold.

As he trudged toward the front door with key in hand, a car parked in the street caught his eye. A medium-sized Japanese car, white, the two men inside in what appeared to be an intense conversation. One of them looked like that weirdo Brenton. Attempting to get a peep without staring, Ryan regarded the other one, whom he didn't recognize. False alarm, then; a case of mistaken identity.

He unlocked the door and sank down in an armchair. Probably just as well he'd been kicked out of the hospital; he needed a shower and hadn't eaten since very early that morning. Christie dominated his thoughts. He'd known of her intense stress but never thought she'd slip over the edge. Witnessing her psychotic state had thrown him into a whirlwind of worry, especially after he'd treated her like crap.

As for his night of drinking which left him paralytic and recovering from a fateful evening spent with a man, he'd succeeded in blocking most of it from his mind. Almost.

Other than the face of the guy, taunting him, leering at him. He'd never considered himself that way. He'd only ever been attracted to women. The thoughts wouldn't go away, the voice in his head demanding answers, asking him how and why he'd woken up in bed with a homosexual man.

Ryan pushed himself up from the armchair and lumbered toward the bathroom. A shower would do him the world of good. Life always got better after sleep. He'd visit Christie and take it from there. Food and sleep would give him the strength he would need to confront whatever the future might bring. He hoped this would make them stronger, bring them closer together. She had to get better; the alternative, well, it sounded all too gruesome. He'd face it tomorrow.

***

Monday 21st January, 8.16pm

"What the hell are you doing here?" said Jake, his voice low and quiet.

"You wouldn't understand," murmured Brenton.

"Give me a break. Let me guess, you wanted just one more glance at Ryan, to be in his space, to sit outside his house and be near him, right?"

Brenton's face fell onto the steering wheel. Jake had told him what he needed to hear. He just couldn't hear it at the time. Breaking up hurt like hell, its searing pain unbearable. He figured that if he could just see Ryan one last time, he could pack away the remnants of his feelings forever, put an end to his obsession and move on.

Ryan had probably forgotten him by now, relegated him to the 'too-hard' basket and got on with life. He needed a reminder. He'd packed what little possessions he would need and withdrawn all the money he had and rented a car, paying cash. When Christie had collapsed, there'd been a flurry of worried figures around her, murmuring and cloistering around her, with hands folded and frowns deepening. His colleagues had been shooed away once the paramedics arrived, and he joined them in speculating about what had happened, whispering sentiments of shock and concern. Truth be known, he'd surprised himself. She was only meant to feel a little bit sick, not collapse. He'd gone too far, given her more than he planned. He should have paid more attention when he emptied the liquid into the plastic bottle to take to work.

Now it was too late. He couldn't go back, no matter how much he wanted to. God, he wished he could explain it to her, the rush of love, the pressure, the anxiety. She'd understand. Shit, he'd ruined his life and hers now.

After an acceptable amount of time had passed and the rubberneckers had returned to their desks, he'd collected his things and left quietly, after speaking to the HR department. He'd told them that as he was a close friend of Christie's, he was struggling to focus, which, with what little remnants of his conscience remained, surprisingly, turned out to be true. Of course, he'd been told to take as much time as he needed, which was just what he needed. He hadn't returned, and didn't intend to. Of course, he'd remained undetected and would probably fade away without a ripple. He flicked his colleague's one last gaze goodbye. He wouldn't miss the rest of them, they were fakers, and lied like a cheap watch. It would be better if he could fix things up on his own.

As Brenton rested his forehead on the steering wheel, his chest tightened and his throat closed. He could lose Ryan forever. With Jake here, he had no chance of sneaking into Ryan's home to plead his case to explain the lengths he'd gone to so they could be together.

His shoulders shook. After a moment, Jake's hand rested on his back.

When the spasms of grief had passed, he sat up and wiped his eyes.

"Drive, let's move further down the street," Jake said.

"What?"

"Ryan might recognize us. The last thing we need is a scene. He's a cop remember? Come on, let's roll the car down."

Brenton shuffled back up into the seat and started the car. He cast a final look inside Ryan's home. "Let's go home," murmured Jake.

Brenton didn't reply.

"We could watch a movie, order a pizza," said Jake. Yet the poison that Brenton had administered to Christie earlier that day did not come up in conversation. Nor did Brenton intend to reveal any of it to Jake. Now that the spreading evil had left him, he was ashamed. Once Jake had left, he'd right the wrongs.

***

Monday 21st January, 11.59pm

Cleaning out the fridge, mopping floors, vacuuming carpets, grocery shopping and cleaning toilets and bathrooms had the desired effect. I flopped onto my bed with a groan. I knew lying down without getting pajamas on first would mean I'd struggle to get back up to change, but I'd had enough. My bones ached, my back tingled and my legs throbbed. As I flung my arms across the bed and closed my eyes, the satisfaction of a clean home and a fully stocked refrigerator lulled me to sleep.

There stood the figure of a dark haired child. Isabella. I'd been so caught up in my furious cleaning project that I'd actually fallen asleep.

—He got to her.

—Yeah, but now not only is Ryan convinced I'm a nutter, but Connor's having doubts too.

—He doesn't realize he will lose her. If this goes on for another day, she will die.

—I get that, but do I have to be the nutter, to lose the man I love to save her? It's too big a sacrifice.

—I can't control Connor's behavior. If he chooses to give in to his fear, then that is his choice to make. Allow him time to make that choice.

—I thought he'd be with me on this. I'm trying to save his daughter.

—Remember, he hasn't told anyone about his gifts as a sentinel. He may never tell. He's struggling.

—Aren't we all! I wonder if all of this is worth it. My conscience is clear, but I might lose any respect or reputation I might have had...

—Only you can answer that, but I appeared to you because I need Christie to live.

—Need, not want? Why?

—That's not important now. It's urgent that you pass on the name of the poison to the hospital so they can administer the antidote in time. They won't check for antifreeze automatically. Keep in mind, though, the hospital staff may not believe you. You'll need to insist they do the test. Once you've done that, you may be able to catch the murderer before he leaves the country.

—Who is he?

—Brenton Perkins. He probably won't be back at work though; he's planning to say one last goodbye to Ryan then he'll be gone.

—And the poison?

—Ethylene Glycol. Antifreeze.

—Antifreeze? As in the stuff that goes in cars?

—Yes. It's sweet. He put it in her coffee Monday. A traceless poison.

—How can it be traceless?

—Well, it can cause a wide range of symptoms. First, the victim seems drunk; afterwards she makes what seems like a miraculous recovery. By day three, if she isn't treated with the antidote, the internal organs go into failure, and she dies.

My throat constricted as I thought of Connor planning his only child's funeral, rather than being torn between loyalty to daughter and lover.

—I need to get to the hospital so they can start tests. They can't treat her otherwise, right?

—Right, but prepare to fight. I don't think you'll be well received.

Maybe not, but every second I stayed, Christie died a little bit more. I could search for this Brenton character in the morning, at dawn. I flicked on the bedside lamp and squinted, adjusting to the bright light. I'd fallen asleep in my tracksuit. The clock beside me read 3.46 a.m. I threw back the covers. I had a job to do, even if I lost Connor because of it. I knew I'd be devastated if it came to that, but if doing the right thing, the honorable thing, ultimately led to our breakup, then the man I'd known as Connor Reardon had never existed at all.

***

Tuesday 22nd January, 12.27am

Connor had dozed fitfully, despite the darkened hospital room and the blanket a thoughtful nurse had draped over him. Nurses had come and gone, checking Christie's blood pressure, smiling at him in the dim light while he tossed and turned, attempting to get comfortable in the hard lumpy old chair.

He scratched the back of his neck and turned on his side, chewing on his lip. He didn't want to think about Christie's future. Thankfully, she slept, blissfully unaware of what the future might bring. Hopefully tomorrow would be a better day. She hadn't been able to keep anything down, and had been put on intravenous fluids to prevent dehydration. Her mental state teetered on the edge. Connor had no idea what he could do other than wait beside her hospital bed, to be a reassuring and familiar presence if she awoke unexpectedly.

He had no idea what might have propelled her into a pit of despair so suddenly. According to colleagues, she'd arrived as usual Monday morning at 8.30, but an hour later she'd begun vomiting and slurring her words. In just a few short hours, she'd descended into madness, hallucinations followed by brief periods of lucidity.

The possibility that Christie had been poisoned seemed unprovable. If Gypsy and her persistent vision of a girl named Isabella really were convinced she had been poisoned, why couldn't they name the poison?

It smelled of attention seeking to Connor. He loved Gypsy; they'd grown closer and he'd come to understand her quirks. Most people strove for integrity, but in Gypsy's case her focus on integrity bordered on obsession. Following purity of principles drove her to irresponsible and reckless behavior. In this case, her dogged determination had carried her through with little to no proof. Their relationship had suffered due to her single mindedness.

He sighed and shifted from his right side to his left. Pulling the blanket up to his chin, he closed his eyes and prayed that the morning would bring an improvement in Christie's condition.

***

Tuesday 22nd January, 3.56am

Brenton awoke to the glowing light of the television credits on an endless loop. He and Jake had fallen asleep just after the movie. He didn't want Jake here. He'd been a great friend, but every second that Jake remained beside him, a faultless friend, meant frustration. He got up and wandered to the light switch. When he flicked it on, Jake blinked and groaned, sitting up on the couch.

"What the hell?"

"Sorry, Jake, but I need to be alone."

Jake brought a wrist to eye level and his lip curled. "At 4 a.m.?"

"Yep, at 4 a.m. You're the best friend a guy could have, and you're always there when I need you, but right now, I need my space. Sorry, Jake."

"Seriously?" said Jake. Brenton's expression remained fixed, hands on hips, waiting close by for him to leave. "Fucking hell then, okay. Hang on; I've got to get my stuff." He pushed out a breath and stood up, grasping for his jacket, shoveling his keys and wallet from the television cabinet into his hands, and shuffling into the hallway.

Jake brought a hand to his head, and he shrugged on his jacket. "Don't do anything stupid, okay? You promised."

"I promise, Jake. Thank you; you've been a great friend. I hope you know how much it means to me."

Jake scrutinized his friend before accepting the hug offered by Brenton. "I'll call you tomorrow in my lunch break," he said before the door slammed shut behind him. Brenton scampered to the window and pressed his nose against the blind, watching as Jake unlocked his car, started it up, and disappeared.

He smiled and swaggered to the lounge room. He hadn't removed the packed bag from the boot of the rental car. He picked up his keys and wallet and stuffed them into his pocket. He'd give it a couple of minutes before he left, in case Jake returned. Then he could carry on with the rest of the plan.

***

Tuesday 22nd January, 4.22am

The roads were deserted. It took only ten minutes to get from my place to St. Vincent's hospital instead of the usual twenty. I swung into a parking space close to the entrance of the Banksia unit. The short beep as I pressed the electronic car lock echoed. I bustled straight for Christie's room. I reached the end of the corridor and I pulled hard on the door to Banksia south, my shoulder jolting back as I realized it wouldn't budge. I searched frantically for a buzzer or intercom. Above the handle, a sign said "Please press for attention."

I slammed it with my palm and stood back, tapping one foot and attempting to peer through the small window in vain, blocked by dark fabric.

I waited for what seemed like an eternity before a stern voice answered, sounding thoroughly unimpressed that a visitor had dared to interrupt the silent ward at four in the morning.

"Yes?"

"Er…I'm here to see Christie Reardon."

"Visiting hours are from 6-8p.m.," said the voice, then a click. Obviously, she considered the subject closed. I pushed the button again, with more ferocity this time.

"Yes?" said a new voice, a gruff-sounding male. Obviously, she'd called in the reinforcements, or the nurse couldn't get to the phone, although at four in the morning I had no idea why not.

"I have vital information concerning Miss Christie Reardon. In fact, it may be a life or death matter."

"Oh yeah?" the young male staff member struggled to keep the skepticism out of his voice.

"Yes. I have received information she may have been poisoned with ethylene glycol or antifreeze, which is the reason her symptoms include hallucinations."

"Right," he said. Obviously, working in a psychiatric ward hadn't improved his view of the public.

"Can I ask you to pass the information on, please? It will probably save her life."

"Is there a reason you want to see her in the middle of the night? It's quarter past four in the morning."

They'd obviously gone on a nationwide recruitment program to find the brightest minds. With a sigh, and pulling out a pen and piece of paper from my handbag, I pushed the point.

"The information has just come to hand. I knew this would make a significant difference to the way she is being treated, which is why I'm here at this time of the night. Ethylene glycol isn't traceable unless it is specifically identified in a urine test."

I'd done my research on the poison, and knew that hospitals wouldn't automatically test for it.

He didn't respond.

I had to get the data through to someone somewhere, medical personnel that actually gave a shit. I scribbled the message in big bold letters, shoved it under the door, and stormed back to the car.

I could call the front desk and get a fax number. The doors swished obediently as I quickened my pace, almost to a run, and bolted for my car.

If the incompetent boobs working in the psychiatric ward didn't act upon the information I'd given them, heads would roll. I'd never trusted psychiatric nurses—you'd have to be nuts to be a psychiatrist and in my experience, most of them were. Of course, as a psychic I'd had my own brushes with psychiatry, which colored my judgment. I'd be damned if I'd let the bastards get hold of Christie. I ran faster. I'd follow this through until they tested Christie and gave her the antidote. Even if they were tired of hearing from me, at least Connor's daughter would live.

***

CHAPTER 11

Chapter Eleven

Tuesday 22nd January, 5.06am

Brenton went back to his car and drove to Ryan's home. He realized he didn't think of it as Christie's place anymore; Ryan featured as the primary figure in his existence. The gorgeous man in question had probably come home to sleep and change, considering it had been almost twenty-four hours since Christie's collapse at work. Brenton estimated that by now, the second day, Christie's demeanor and physical symptoms would have transformed from a seemingly drunk delusional woman into a calmer, rapidly improving one.

Somehow, this made him feel better, less guilty. Ryan and Connor would be thankful that Christie perked up and their worst fears could be relegated to needless worry. He'd given that to them, the knowledge that life and health were precious. He smiled at the rear of Ryan's car in the driveway. He'd be up with the sparrows, keen to check on his girlfriend and wait patiently by her side. Brenton reclined back in the seat to wait for him to surface.

Brenton knew Ryan better than he knew himself.

He let the car roll down the hill slightly, but then, Ryan wouldn't recognize his rental vehicle, nor would he recognize his pale features in the growing light of pre-dawn. Ryan certainly would never imagine that Brenton had set up outside his home—a bright side to the unfortunate fact that Brenton didn't register as a major figure in Ryan's world.

Yet.

***

Tuesday 22nd January, 5.36am

I plonked my body onto my office chair with such force that it skidded about a meter before I scooted forward, grabbing the phone off my desk.

I dialed the hospital number and it seemed to ring for an eternity. Surely, the receptionists weren't run off their feet at five a.m.

"St. Vincent's Hospital." The woman answering sounded as though another second taking another call and she'd hurl her nail polish bottle across the room.

"Yes, I'd like the fax number and email for the Banksia unit, if possible, please." I kept my tone brisk and professional, confident of getting the help I needed to resolve this for the last time.

"Hold, please—" and with a click, the torturous clanging chimes of hold music began.

A bird ripped a worm from the earth outside, smacking it against the hard earth.

"Are you there?"

"Yes," I replied. I sure as hell didn't plan to board a plane to the Bahamas anytime soon.

"The fax number is 9238 6566. Emails will need to come via reception." I scribbled the details down and hung up, frantically searching for signs of life on my laptop. I opened my email program and began to type the message, which I planned to send as a fax first before duplicating on all possible channels.

−URGENT − Patient in Banksia Ward − Christie Reardon − have received vital information regarding her condition − suspect Brenton Perkins, work colleague, administered poison Monday morning 9.30 a.m. − Ethylene Glycol. Police have been informed. Should an organ or blood donor be needed, please discuss with Connor Reardon, a frequent visitor and her biological father.

I printed my message, slotted the paper into the fax machine, and pressed 'send.' I pushed myself up from the chair and grabbed my keys. No chance of sleep yet, but my body needed rest. I wasn't too worried; I'd slept the night before. A walk around the block, then I'd retreat to my bedroom for the next round in the battle against insomnia.

If the blanket of sleep did overcome me, Isabella could confirm that I'd averted disaster. In the morning, I could go vermin hunting for this Brenton character.

***

Tuesday 22nd January, 6.51am

Grit stung Ryan's eyes as they flickered open. As he sat up, he realized he'd fallen asleep in a towel. He hadn't fully grasped the level of his exhaustion. At the window, he twisted the cord to open the blinds and the gray clear sky lightened the room a little.

Dressing rapidly, he bounded down the stairs toward the kitchen where he found his keys and wallet piled on the table. He'd get breakfast on the way. He had a good feeling about today. Christie, he hoped, would be improved, sitting up in bed, smiling in her familiar way, the shy grin spreading across her face.

He realized he'd been an asshole lately, but ever since that dickhead had lodged a formal complaint with the department, the slightest annoyance had left him teetering on the edge of fury. He knew he'd been too hard on Christie, but waking up in that idiot's home on Sunday morning had frightened him. He couldn't recall any of the drunken events, so that had to count for something, didn't it? Those trashy TV shows would have a field day with something like this—the gossipy B-list celebrity women loved to chew over this type of thing, spending hours dissecting meaningless drivel.

No, he knew he hadn't been hiding in a closet, and he didn't plan to leave one anytime soon.

He swung the door open and stepped briskly toward the car. Getting in, he reversed quickly. Christie and Connor would be waiting for him.

***

Tuesday 22nd January, 8.09am

Christie awoke and pushed herself up to get her bearings. Her limbs ached, and the faint twinge of a headache had formed at the base of her skull.

Christie noticed the equipment on the wall and smelled disinfectant. She was in a hospital. As she sighed and sank back onto the bed, the collapse at work came back to her—she had struggled against the waves of nausea, the shame and humiliation of possibly throwing up at work, the spinning room, struggling to speak, the dribbling, before falling off her chair.

Oh god.

What happened? It had been a Monday like any other. She knew she hadn't been drinking. Did someone really get to her? Connor's crazy girlfriend kept on banging on about poisoning, but she had felt fine, other than a slight headache. She did, however, remember the nightmares. Vivid memories of gray-green creatures tapping at the windows, squeaking and scurrying across the floor, climbing and slithering their way in through gaps in windows and under doors.

She shivered and ran her fingers through her hair. It felt greasy; she really needed a shower. A nurse peered around the door and smiled at her.

"Good morning. You seem to be doing better today." Her voice was barely a whisper but she did look genuinely pleased to see her up in bed. She padded over and slid a blood pressure cuff onto Christie's arm. Connor shifted in the chair, gazing left and right as he got his bearings. When he noticed Christie was awake, he smiled and threw off the blanket.

"Christie," he said his voice gruff with sleep.

"Connor," she said, smiling as he stood and shuffled his way to her bedside.

The nurse addressed her again. "You can probably have a shower this morning, seeing as you're doing so much better. I've been told to collect a urine specimen from you—the doctors ordered another test."

Christie picked up the plastic bottle, peering at it.

"So I can have a shower then?"

"Of course you can, if I can just get that urine specimen first. I'll get you a couple of towels. The doctor will be making his rounds in a few hours. He can update you more then." With a quick swish of the bed covers, the nurse left.

Connor took her hand resting on the bed, and held it in his. His fingers were a little rough, but warm and comforting as they rubbed her palm.

"How are you feeling? You look a lot better today."

"I remember feeling really sick at work. I thought I'd vomit at my desk—it was horrible. Then I had these freaky nightmares, about slimy creatures at the door and windows, trying to get in to attack me. What happened to me?"

"You were vomiting and slept a lot. Sometimes you said things that made sense, other times…not so much."

"Oh god, how embarrassing." Christie brought her hands up to cover her face. "What did I say? Oh, shit…don't tell me."

"Nothing too incriminating; don't worry. I'm just glad you're okay." Connor sat on the edge of her bed. "Although you did scream at Gypsy, calling her an evil witch and yelled at her for torturing your brother."

"That won't help relations." Christie swung the bedcovers aside. The hospital room door opened and Ryan stood in the doorway.

"Ryan!" Christie flung her arms out in greeting. Ryan rushed toward her and wrapped her in a hug, whispering into her shoulder, "Thank God you're okay. I'm so glad. I love you so much."

When Ryan pulled away, Christie brushed tears from her face. "I'm so sorry, I had no idea."

"I'll bet." Ryan's expression relaxed and color began to return to his face.

"I've been asked to pee in this cup. After that, I'll have a shower. I'll be back soon." Christie pushed herself up off the bed and shuffled toward the bathroom.

When the door had closed behind her, Connor spoke quietly. "I was worried there for a while."

"I'll never take her for granted again."

Connor took a tentative step toward Ryan. "Ryan, the staff did do a test for poison in Christie's blood? For certain?"

"Apparently they did—I asked them to. They tested for the usual heavy metals, arsenic, mercury, lead, and she got the all clear. She hasn't been poisoned." Ryan sank down onto the unmade bed.

"I'm just wondering what caused this, that's all. I know she's been under stress, but the vomiting and hallucinations takes things to a whole new level."

"I know. They'll probably discharge her soon. I wouldn't be surprised if she gets moved to another ward shortly." Ryan's phone buzzed in his pocket and he let it ring.

"I think I'll grab a quick coffee. Won't be long," said Connor.

As Connor reached the door, Ryan put a hand out to him. "Have you had any sleep recently?"

"No. Wouldn't hurt, I guess."

"It looks like Christie will be home soon, anyway. Get some sleep."

"I will. Thanks, Ryan."

Connor headed down the corridor. As he passed the nurses' station, a young male nurse stepped into the corridor.

"Mr. Reardon? Connor Reardon," said the nurse. "I wonder if I could have a quiet word please, in private."

***

Tuesday 22nd January, 7.21am

Brenton watched as Ryan took off, waiting a minute or two before getting out of the car. There were two other houses nearby, but large trees blocked his vision.

He stepped through the front garden, giving the windows a quick nudge to determine whether they had been unlocked. He looked in to see if anyone was inside. Empty. As he reached the side of the property, he noticed an old-fashioned window frame, one he could prise open. *Perfect.*

The side of the house was in shade, with quite a few bushes flowering, which meant he would be hidden, and the window level would allow easy access. Flicking a glance left and right, he latched on to the frame and levered one leg up and over, and in less than a minute, he reached what appeared to be a laundry.

Brenton paced through the house, scrutinizing each room, opening cupboards and examining their contents. He found clothes, shoes, toiletries and underwear. He imagined Ryan eating his breakfast, chatting to Christie. He had deliberately left the bedroom until last. The room where Ryan slept and changed would be his favorite.

He noticed the carpet changed color, and a sweet waft of aftershave reached his nose. He was close. The bed was unmade and clothing in various shapes and sizes had been flung across the floor.

Brenton swept a hand across the sheets, hoping that maybe they would still be warm. No luck. He fell backward onto the bed, rubbing his arms across the bed linen. As he breathed in and smiled, he thought he detected the faint scent of deodorant and soap. Ryan had slept here.

As he lay there inhaling Ryan's scent, his gaze was caught by a bright red t-shirt lying on the floor next to a pair of khaki shorts. He raised himself up from the bed, and picked up the two items, inhaling their fragrance. The distinct aroma of Ryan washed over him. He fell back on the bed with eyes closed, carefully arranging the clothes across his body. He imagined how it would feel to have Ryan moving across him, brushing his fingers against his skin. As Brenton's fantasy took over, his breathing slowed and he relaxed.

***

Tuesday 22nd January, 7.50am

I returned from my power walk with a thin film of sweat across my skin and made straight for the shower, hoping that afterwards I'd be fortunate and get some sleep. Surely, Isabella would be aware of Brenton's location. If she'd seen him preparing the poison and administering it to Christie, she should know if the slimy worm had left the country.

I'd love to get my hands on him, sneaky little prick.

Interesting, though, that Ryan had gone home with two men Saturday night. The mask that many people adopted as a public persona, particularly those that worked in the service of others, could be quite a revelation. I wondered what mask Ryan wore, and if he had ever considered himself bisexual? Although Isabella had told me he hadn't slept with either of them, he didn't know that yet. Still, Ryan's protests made sense in light of what he thought he'd got up to with Brenton. Justification could be a powerful thing, particularly if a person had things he'd rather left unsaid. Christie, of course, remained none the wiser. I wouldn't be doing myself any favors if I were the one to tell her what I knew. I'd leave that to Ryan to disclose at some point in the future, if ever.

Drying myself, I headed for the bedroom, looking forward to snuggling down into the warmth of my mattress, even if the early morning light made its way through the blinds. I lay on the bed, staring up at the ceiling, wishing for a revelation: the location of Brenton Perkins.

After over an hour of tossing and turning with no sign of Isabella, I realized it wouldn't happen. I threw back the covers and began to get dressed. I'd head back to the hospital. Maybe by now they'd tested her and treated Christie with the antidote.

Tuesday 22nd January, 9.55am

The nurse seemed nervous. He rubbed his hands together, and his mouth opened and closed like a fish.

"Mr. Reardon, I'm not sure how to bring this up. It's a rather delicate subject."

"I'm on my way home. How about you dive right in and say it?"

The nurse pulled open a drawer beside the desk. "We received this today after an early morning visit from a woman named Gypsy. She insisted we conduct tests to determine ethylene glycol levels in Ms. Reardon's blood, but I, er, wanted to speak to you about the other matter."

Connor read the fax. *Gypsy.* She'd gone over his head.

"The fax was sent by a friend of mine, Gypsy Shields. I'll take this up with her. She's not a complete crackpot. I think a test would be a good idea, just to eliminate it as a possibility." Connor rose from his seat.

"Please, Mr. Reardon. I wanted to clarify. Is there any substance to her claim that you are Ms. Reardon's biological father?"

"It's never been proven by a paternity test, if that's what you're getting at. But Gypsy is convinced I'm Christie's father."

"Would you like a paternity test done?"

Connor rubbed his chin. "I guess if you're willing to do so. It would certainly explain a few things." He wondered if he really wanted to force the issue. He decided he did, if it meant saving Christie's life.

"We'll conduct both tests and put an urgent rush on them. Stay in touch, Mr. Reardon. We may need your assistance."

"You can count on it," Connor said over his shoulder as he strode away.

He headed for the car with his hands squeezed into fists and heat rising up from his throat. Gypsy had some explaining to do.

***

Tuesday 22nd January, 10.21am

Christie was sitting up in bed with Ryan standing by her side when the doctor arrived on his rounds.

"Ms. Reardon, good morning."

Christie smiled at him. "Good morning, doctor. Any news?"

"Well, obviously you're doing much better today. In fact, so much better that you'll be moved to another ward in the next hour or so."

Ryan took a step forward. "Moved? To where?"

"The Banksia unit is no longer appropriate for your needs. You'll be moved to probably Two North, a more general medical ward. We're awaiting a final test. Then with a bit of luck, you'll be discharged in the next 24 hours or so." The doctor removed his hands from his pockets.

"Sounds great," Christie said, reaching for Ryan's hand. "What sort of test are you doing?"

The doctor shuffled his feet and cleared his throat before speaking. "We believe your coffee Monday morning may have been tampered with, the additive of something quite specific and which hasn't been tested for yet. We've put a rush on the results and should have them in an hour or so. We'll let you know as soon as we know."

"Poison?" said Christie, flicking a glance at Ryan.

"Possibly. We received information that you may have been given a specific poison. One that is traceless unless specifically searched for. As I said, we'll have information on the test results in an hour or so. In the meantime, someone will be here shortly to transfer you to another ward. You're doing nicely, though. I honestly don't think you'll be with us for longer than another day."

Christie glanced at Ryan. "So she might have been right."

"Maybe." Ryan's voice was low and dangerous, and he spoke through clenched teeth. Christie considered this for a moment, then threw back the covers on the bed and placed her feet on the cold hospital linoleum floor.

The doctor watched them. "Is there anything I should know?"

"No, no," said Christie and Ryan almost in unison, and Christie laughed nervously. She wriggled on the bed as she stood up. "I'm pretty keen to move wards, though. I'd better have a shower and start packing my belongings."

"Good idea. Someone will be along to help you in an hour or so. As soon as we have the results, we'll let you know."

The doctor left the room, his shoes clacking on the polished linoleum floor.

"Good news, then." Christie turned to Ryan, who had fixed his gaze on his shoes. "Come on help me pack my stuff up."

***

CHAPTER 12

Chapter Twelve

Tuesday 22nd January, 11.19am

I'd managed to get an hour or two of sleep. Better than nothing, I guess. I threw back the covers and headed toward the drawers, rummaging through them to find socially acceptable clothes. I'd just begun dressing when I heard the click of the front door.

Probably Connor.

I abandoned the shower idea, turning off the water, and reached for a robe. The door jolted open, and there in the doorway stood Connor, muscles rigid, teeth clenched and the blood flushing his face. What the hell?

"Connor," I said.

"How dare you. Of all the nerve!" Connor's deep voice reverberated through the bathroom.

"I need to get dressed. What's wrong with you?"

"You told the nursing staff that I was Christie's father. You had no right." He clenched and unclenched his fists.

I stepped into my underwear and glared at Connor. "Of all people, you don't believe that anyone could possibly poison Christie. Yet if anything happens to her, you don't want to have that conversation with anyone. What if she needs a blood transfusion? What will you do then? All care, no responsibility, right?"

"It wasn't your place to say anything. You know that." He spat the words through clenched teeth, but his voice sounded childish and sulky to my ear.

"I am so over this! You're telling me that you're too afraid to tell Christie you might be her father? Have you ever considered she'd be overjoyed to *have* a father, considering she thought she lost him years ago?" I stepped into my jeans.

"Like I said, it's none of your business."

"You're kidding, right? None of my business? Some spirit appears to warn me that Christie's life is in danger, and that if a blood or organ donor is needed in an emergency, you fit the bill. In spite of all of that, you aren't sure? My god, with your abilities I always thought you were in my corner, that you had my back. It sounds like you don't believe me anymore."

Connor turned away, tightening his fists before returning to face me. I began brushing my hair.

"This is big news, and damn it, this is private! How do you think I felt when some stranger, some young nursing graduate, asked me about Christie's paternity? Do you think you could have given me a heads-up, some idea that you'd told the hospital staff about this?"

"No, I don't!" I said, and threw the hairbrush on the bed in disgust. "You forced the issue, Connor. What's so scary that you can't have a conversation with Christie? What's the worst that can happen? Do you really think she'll stop talking to you over something like this? Do you think she'll be upset that you kept the secret from her? Seriously?"

The muscles in Connor's jaw were twitching almost uncontrollably. I knew the look. It meant that Connor had reined in his temper as much as possible and was reaching his limits.

"Why, Gypsy? Do you really want me have a conversation like this with Christie? Why can't it stay a secret?"

"Hell Connor! You think *I* forced the issue. Seriously? I was a messenger, nothing more, nothing less. I can't control Christie and Ryan's reaction, just as I can't control yours. Somehow, I'm the bad guy. Christie resents me, pure and simple. I'm not surprised, when she's been visiting her weasel fucking brother in jail—of course she hates me!"

"Stay away from Christie. You're making things worse!"

"I'm trying to save her life." My voice sounded shrill and hysterical to my ears. I couldn't believe this. When faced with a choice between his psychopathic nephew and me, he'd chosen me. He'd supported me, helping me deal with the fallout after Aaron not only tried to kill me but also broke into my home. I'd always thought I could count on Connor's support no matter what. It seemed my confidence was misplaced.

Connor stormed out of the room and stomped downstairs. I heard the bang of drawers in what sounded like the hallway cupboard.

I bounded down the stairs.

Connor panted as he ripped items from the cupboard, flinging them across the hallway floor.

"What are you doing?"

"What does it look like I'm doing? Packing a bag."

"Has it really come to this?"

My heart, which hammered in my chest, kicked up a notch. We'd got through the argument with Christie and Ryan, and so I'd never thought he'd leave me, ever. Connor packing a bag seemed unreal, impossible.

Ice filled my veins and I reached out to touch Connor's shoulder.

"Don't do this, Connor. Not now. Don't be stupid. We're already under a lot of pressure."

He shrugged my hand away. "I need time to think. I'm checking into a hotel." He'd found a faded green duffle bag and dragged it behind him up the stairs.

"This is ridiculous! Stop, Connor, we can work this out. We've been through worse than this." I followed him, my breath coming in short gasps. Connor either didn't hear me or completely ignored my pleas.

When I entered the room, half of the closet's contents were strewn across the floor.

I gave a valiant last attempt to make him stay, seizing his arm, but he simply shrugged away from my grasp.

"Where will you stay?" I said.

"I don't know. There's a motel nearby. I'll see if they have any vacancies." His head was down and he wouldn't meet my eyes.

"So what, are we breaking up? Somehow I never imagined it would come to this."

"Me neither," he said. He stuffed the items into the bag and zipped it up. "I'll be in touch." And just like that, he headed out of the room.

"Why don't you sleep on it? And if you're really serious about leaving, you can take your stuff first thing in the morning."

Connor hung his head, the scruffy old duffle bag hanging forlornly in his left hand.

"Goodbye, Gypsy," he mumbled, and he closed the bedroom door behind him.

I listened to his feet bounding down the stairs, the front door opening and slamming closed. He unlocked the boot, threw in the bag with a thud, and started the car up. Within seconds, he reversed the car out of the driveway and the silence enveloped me, almost deafening.

In the blink of an eye, Connor exited my life.

When I spoke to Isabella the previous day, she had told me that if Connor left me over this then he wasn't the man I thought he was. I'd never believed that he'd leave me, ever, and certainly not over something like this.

As the realization dawned on me, the ice in my veins reached my chest. My knees buckled and I landed on the bedroom floor. Tears flowed freely, with no one to see them.

I pounded my fist on the ground and the hot tears fell faster.

Connor and I were finished.

CHAPTER 13

Chapter Thirteen

Tuesday 22nd January, 12.31pm

Christie's eyes were open wide as the orderly wheeled her down the busy corridor. Ryan held her hand, and they turned left, making for the lift to reach their destination, ward two.

"Something's wrong, Ryan."

"What?" Ryan lowered his chin and he gazed at Christie, to see her complexion a pasty gray. "What's going on? Talk to me."

"It's my pulse. My heart's banging so hard, and I can't—I can't breathe properly."

Christie's breath really did sound raspy, and her eyes were wide. Ryan called out to the hospital orderly. "Can something be done? She says she can't breathe properly, she's distressed."

The orderly pressed a button on the side of the bed rail.

"I'm sorry; I'm going to have to ask you to meet us up there. I'm going to call in the team." The orderly's fingers were resting on Christie's wrist. "We're going upstairs. The staff there will help her."

Ryan remained at the edge of the corridor, unmoving, as she was whisked away from him with a burst of intense speed.

God, he hoped she would be okay. Ryan flicked the sweat off his brow and sat down on a plastic chair. He pulled out his phone and sent a text to Connor. *Something's wrong, Christie has been rushed off for treatment. Get to the hospital ASAP.*

***

Tuesday 22nd January, 12.33pm

Gypsy curled in the fetal position on the bedroom floor, gasping to get her breath through her tears. A loud, confident voice burst into her head.

–Gypsy, get up!

– Leave me alone, Renee.

– What are you doing on the floor? Get up, Christie needs you.

–Go away. It's none of my business anymore. I tried to help, but it hasn't done any good. Connor's gone.

In her bedroom, Renee shook her head. She'd have to snap her aunt out of this, and fast.

—*Isabella visited me again. We need your help. Brenton is stalking Ryan.* Renee's voice sounded clear and confident. This taking charge business was becoming a habit.

—*He's a nutcase…*

Renee watched with satisfaction as Gypsy pushed herself up from the floor and walked over with wobbly legs to collapse on the bed.

—*Brenton's been parking his rental car outside Ryan and Christie's place. He's packed a bag, ready to do a runner, but before he does, he hopes he'll convince Ryan to come with him.*

—*What about Christie?*

—*The hospital staff weren't sure about your message at first. They thought you were a random nutter, until they spoke to Connor and he agreed that Christie might have been poisoned with antifreeze. So they've done tests.*

—*Thank god someone is listening.*

Renee's heart rate was racing, almost exploding. She hadn't wanted to get involved, but after another visit from Isabella, she knew she had to. Renee licked her lips. She wanted to run away and hide, curl up in her bed. Maybe after this was all over, she could.

—*Just in time, too. Christie's heart is beginning to fail. The poison is affecting her internal organs.*

Isabella says they'll get the antidote to her soon, though. She should make it.

—So what's being done about this Brenton crackpot?

—Nothing at the moment, but then he's only just crossed the line. Yesterday he sat outside Ryan's home, but luckily, his friend Jake convinced him to go home. Today, though—he broke in.

Renee suppressed a cry. She wanted to scream, but that wouldn't help. Gypsy would sort it out, but that didn't stop her heart from banging in her chest like a runaway train.

— Oh my god…

—Isabella is worried it could get nasty if Ryan goes home and finds him. Brenton is lying in their bed, and has Ryan's clothes draped across him. He's fallen asleep.

Gypsy felt a creeping sensation across her skin.

—I knew Brenton had problems, but this is ridiculous. I'm going over there.

—Not yet. Isabella wants you to talk to Connor first.

—I don't think Connor wants to talk to me. He said he needed time to think.

—Isabella said that later tonight the hospital would verify that you were right. The doctor will be talking to Connor and Ryan then. Once Connor realizes the mistake he's made, he'll be more willing to listen.

−I need to go over there.

−No! Brenton's still loose. Wait! Christie is okay for now, but she could yet be in more danger. You still have to convince Connor to listen to you. Just wait.

Renee broke the connection, and Gypsy threw herself back on the bed. She hoped that the separation from Connor would be temporary, not permanent.

***

Tuesday 22nd January, 1.38pm

Ryan sat on the plastic chair in the hospital corridor, face gray, his forearms resting on his legs. Footsteps clicked to his right, and raising his head, he saw Connor arrive.

"Connor."

He placed one arm lightly on Ryan's shoulder. "I came as soon as I heard. How is she?"

"They said they weren't quite sure. They need to run more tests. They whisked her away after her heart rate went up and she struggled to breathe. Then I heard an announcement over the speakers, saying 'code blue,' and I wondered if it was for her."

"She'll be fine, mate."

"I don't know what to think. All I know is I want Christie back. I'm even wondering if Gypsy was right and we were too quick to judge her.

Maybe Christie has been poisoned. Nothing else explains it."

"We'll find out when the doctor arrives. How about a coffee?"

"I guess." Ryan ran his fingers through his hair. "Maybe if I'd done things differently, things would have been different—Christie would be safe."

"How do you figure that? Come on, let's go." Connor stood and beckoned Ryan to follow.

"A coffee won't hurt. Maybe we could check in with the doctors when we get back."

"Good idea."

CHAPTER 14

Chapter Fourteen

Tuesday 22nd January, 2.26pm

Brenton woke up, smiled and ran his hands over the sheets. He could smell Ryan everywhere, in the closet, on the bedding. He didn't want to leave, nor did he want to think about what might happen if Ryan discovered him.

He decided he'd have another look around, get to know Ryan a bit more. He started with the bathroom cupboards, discovering wonders such as shaving cream, gel and razor blades, but no medications that he could see. Brenton had been on antidepressants for a while. He hated the dullness they gave him, but they seemed to keep him from dangerous lows. He wondered if either Christie or Ryan took them, but it didn't look like it.

As he stood up, he heard chimes echoing throughout the hallway. Someone was ringing the doorbell. Shit. Brenton stood still, barely daring to breathe, waiting for the unexpected caller to give up and step away from the front door. He hadn't left his car in the driveway, so there was nothing to give away his presence.

The doorbell rang again.

It was probably just a door-to-door sales person and so Brenton ignored it, and continued rifling through the bathroom cupboards, hoping for a gem, some discovery that would give him insight into Ryan's life. Nothing.

The mystery caller had started knocking on the door, quietly at first, then louder.

He heard footsteps shuffling on the front porch, then a voice.

"Brenton. Brent! Are you in there? Open the door!"

Jake had found him. He tried ignoring him for a while longer, but the foot shuffling and knocking began again, even louder this time.

The knocking became pounding. If he didn't answer it soon, one of the neighbors might hear the commotion and do something about it.

Brenton ran to the front door and opened it. There was Jake, red-faced, out of breath, and wild-eyed.

Jake pushed his way in and slammed the door shut. "What the hell are you thinking? You know breaking and entering is illegal, right?"

He turned away. "Give it a rest, Jake. I didn't damage the place. One of the windows was open, almost like someone wanted me to get in."

"Okay, you've officially lost your mind. Let's get out of here, *now*."

Brenton crossed his arms. He wouldn't be going anywhere. It was time for Jake to leave.

"The only reason I let you in is because you were making too much noise. It's time for you to leave."

"One of us needs to see sense. Come on, let's go, we won't talk about it again. If the cops find out about this, it'll get ugly. You'll be arrested."

Brenton headed toward the couch and threw himself onto it. "Too late for that."

Jake hesitated before joining Brenton on the couch. "What do you mean, too late?"

When Brenton didn't reply, he spoke again, going pale. "Oh god, what have you done?"

Brenton smiled. "Nothing too major. Just spiked his girl's drink with a little something."

"Are you completely mad? You spiked her drink? With what?"

"A little something I found in the garage." Brenton wiped his hands on his jeans.

"Like poison, you mean? What the hell have you done?" Jake pushed himself up from the chair and stormed toward Brenton, grabbed his shoulders and began shaking him. Brenton threw up an arm to knock him away.

"Get your hands off me!" Brenton's breath escaped in short gasps.

"I don't believe this! Not only have you broken into his house, but you've poisoned his girlfriend! Every second that I'm here, I'm an accessory now. You know that, right?"

"I didn't ask you to come." Brenton would no longer look at his friend. Instead, his gaze fixed firmly on the floor.

"No you didn't. I came because I'm your friend—not that I think you even understand what a real friend is. God knows you don't deserve any friends, not after this. We could both end up in jail."

"You're free to leave whenever you please. If you're so worried about ending up in jail, then go. There's no way anyone will know it was me; the poison I used is colorless and completely untraceable. Of course, I had planned on telling the hospital the name of the poison, anonymously of course."

"But why? Why did you do this? It's madness!" Jake's voice sounded hysterical and he flailed his hands around.

Brenton covered his face with his hands and began to cry. Jake stopped pacing the room, ran his hands through his hair, and swore softly. He kneeled in front of Brenton.

Brenton began to speak but Jake couldn't make out what he was saying.

"Brent," he said softly, "slow down, I can't understand a word you're saying. Breathe in, and out."

As Jake spoke, Brenton took short, sharp breaths and his shoulders heaved.

"I'm sorry. It wasn't meant to be like this. It's just Ryan, he's the *one*."

Jake rested his hand on Brenton's shoulder. "We can still make this right. Let's call the hospital, then the police."

Brenton hiccupped and blew his nose. "I want you to know, Jake, it was never meant to be like this. I planned on making the call before now, it all got out of control and before I knew it–"

"I know, I know." Jake's voice was soothing, quiet. "We need to talk to someone now, we can't wait, and I don't want anything to happen to her." He stood up and pulled his phone out of his back pocket.

He heard a car pull up, then footsteps across the driveway to the front porch. He froze, his gaze fixed on Brenton.

"Who's that?" whispered Brenton, eyes wide. A key turned in the lock, and the door creaked, as it swung open. Ryan stood in the hallway, fury written across his face.

***

Tuesday 22nd January, 5.15pm

Christie couldn't pinpoint the exact moment when she fell asleep. She remembered her heart banging so hard in her chest she thought it would burst through, and she remembered desperately sucking in each ragged painful breath. She remembered being surrounded by people, barking out orders at each other and wheeling over equipment. Ryan and Connor were nowhere to be seen.

Drowsiness overcame her, sleep pulling her down. She had tried to force her eyes to stay open, but it was impossible. She drifted off, and in her dreams, she found herself in a darkened room with light streaming in through the windows. The slimy creatures and monsters of earlier nightmares were gone. A hand smoothed her hair, and she turned to see her mother and father beside her.

"Mum, Dad," she whispered, unable to say much more than that. Her throat closed over, and hot tears welled in her eyes.

"Shh, honey, it's okay. We wanted to let you know we're here for you."

Christie wondered why they were here. Did this mean she'd already died? She'd heard about near death experiences and people being drawn to the light and seeing dead loved ones. She tried to open her mouth to ask her parents what was happening, where her grandfather was, but no words came out.

She closed her eyes and smiled as her mother continued to stroke her hair. It took her back to her childhood, when Dad had been alive. Life was so different then; Mum wasn't drinking and she actually paid attention to them. After her father had died in the explosion, everything had been different.

The hair stroking was sending her back to sleep. She realized that falling asleep inside a dream seemed weird. She felt a pinch on her arm.

"Wake up."

Christie opened her eyes slowly. Beside her bed was a child, a girl maybe 9 or 10 years old with long brown hair and a serious face, studying her intently.

"It's not time to go to sleep yet, wake up."

Christie opened her mouth in a second attempt to speak, but was unsuccessful.

"It's okay, you don't need to talk. I can read your thoughts. For now, all you need to know is that I'm a friend. It's not your time yet—if you do sleep, stay away from the light."

Stay away from the light?

The young girl's gaze did not leave Christie. "For now, you need to rest. Don't worry you'll see Ryan and Connor again."

Christie let out a long breath, and wondered if it would be okay to sleep. Isabella nodded at her, and she drifted downward into unconsciousness.

***

Tuesday 22nd January, 6.01pm

Ryan and Connor arrived back at the ward and hovered around the nurses' station. Connor spoke first.

"Hello. We're the family of Christie Reardon. Could we have a word with a doctor, please?"

The dark-haired nurse smiled at them. "Certainly, he'll be with you shortly. Have a seat."

Connor and Ryan resumed their position on the rickety plastic orange chairs in the corridor. Ryan jiggled a foot on the linoleum floor and Connor rubbed his chin. Within minutes, a tall gray-haired man in a suit appeared at the station and conferred quietly with the nurses. He flicked a glance over at Ryan and Connor. They both rose as he approached them with clicking heels. "I'm Dr. McKenzie. I thought you'd like an update on Christie's progress."

"Please, yes, we'd appreciate it," said Connor, removing his hands from his pockets.

"Christie is currently in ICU, where she's getting the best care available."

"Intensive care? What happened?"

"She struggled for a while, but she's stable now."

Ryan rubbed a hand across the stubble on his chin, and slowly sat back down. "What happened to her? Will she be okay?"

"She'll be fine now. Unfortunately, we weren't aware that her internal organs were going into failure, but then, that's the nature of the substance she was given."

The doctor's lip curled and he shook his head.

"Poison?"

"We were advised, as you may remember, Mr. Reardon, that Christie may have been poisoned with ethylene glycol. When we conducted further tests, we discovered the crystals in her system. She's been given the antidote."

Ryan covered his face with his hands, and Connor began pacing.

Connor pulled in his brows and swallowed hard. The news meant serious implications. Gypsy had been right all along, and he'd doubted her, of all people, *he'd doubted her*.

"The poison is unique in that it is traceless unless specifically tested for, and its effects mimic symptoms of other diseases. More specifically, her vomiting and hallucinations during the first 12 hours were the poison taking effect."

Connor sat down, gripping the side of the chair.

Connor hadn't been prepared for Gypsy being right. He'd been so convinced that Christie would be fine, and that Isabella and Gypsy were wrong, that he'd nearly lost his daughter. He didn't know if she'd forgive him, or even where to start.

"Her seemingly miraculous recovery on the second day was part of the poison making its way through her system. Although she appeared well, at that point her organs were being damaged one by one. If the poison had continued its journey through her body, she would have suffered kidney failure, heart failure then death."

Ryan took a step closer to the doctor, leaning forward. "How long ago was she given the antidote?"

"We rushed the antidote to her as soon as the test results came through a couple of hours ago. She's resting comfortably. It's a waiting game now, I'm afraid, to see how she recovers."

Ryan blew out a breath.

"Any ideas on how long?" said Ryan.

The doctor shoved his hands back in his pockets. "Unfortunately, there's no way of knowing. We are monitoring her closely, though, she's in good hands. By this time tomorrow we'll know more."

Connor's mouth opened and closed, but no words came.

Ryan's shoulders sagged. "Could it be a matter of hours?"

"Probably not. Now would be a good time to get some rest. Tomorrow morning we'll definitely know more. Christie is getting the very best care available, that I can promise you."

Connor pushed hair out of his eyes and spoke softly. "Thank you doctor, you've saved Christie's life. We appreciate what you did, more than I can tell you."

"Don't thank me. Thank the person who notified us of the poison. Without that information, we may have had a different outcome today."

Connor covered his face in his hands. "Gypsy," he whispered. "I'll be here again tomorrow to see how she's doing. Take care," the doctor said, before his heels clicked down the corridor.

Ryan moved across to the chair nearest Connor. "What's your take on all that?"

"I'm numb" mumbled Connor, not looking at Ryan.

"I keep thinking about Gypsy, how I treated her. I wouldn't blame her if she never spoke to me again. She saved Christie's life."

"Gypsy's not like that. She'll forgive, I hope. She'll be relieved that Christie actually made it. I'll send her a message. "

A rush of adrenaline surged through Connor, and a sudden coldness crept up his back. He'd been so sure Gypsy had it wrong, so sure that Christie would be fine, that he'd disregarded all of her information, and he'd left her. Why did he doubt her like that?

The truth of the matter was that he didn't want to reveal the family secret, he wasn't sure if he was ready. He'd paid a private visit to the nurse, and asked if a paternity test had been conducted. The results were back, he really was Christie's father, and he didn't quite know how to face it.

His blind spot surrounding Christie had nearly cost him his relationship. He prided himself on his integrity, his loyalty, but this time his instincts had let him down.

And Gypsy. When she'd needed him, he'd abandoned her. She'd been right—of anyone, he should have been there for her, he who understood her abilities, who knew the highs and the lows of visions and the psychic world. His discomfort as a sentinel, combined with his unwillingness to confront whether he was Christie's father had meant his relationship with Gypsy had shattered and splintered.

He hoped he could make it up to her.

"I'm going to take a walk, Ryan, okay?" he said, retrieving his mobile phone from a jacket pocket.

"Yeah, take your time," muttered Ryan.

Connor pushed up from the chair and headed down the corridor toward the double doors. As they swung behind him, he saw a flurry of activity in the hospital foyer, and instead he made for the gardens at the rear of the building. He needed some space, some quiet time to take it all in.

As Connor passed the cafeteria, he saw the chapel through a doorway to his right. Connor had never considered himself religious, but the quiet sanctity of the quiet space seemed soothing and peaceful, just what he needed.

The room, complete with stained glass windows and three rows of seating, was hushed and deserted. He took a seat at the front pew, head falling into his hands. He noticed his fingers had stopped shaking and he blew out a long breath. Connor relaxed a little and sat back in the chair. He sensed movement to his right, and saw a minister sitting further along the pew.

"Welcome," said the minister. He looked to be in his late sixties, and as he smiled the wrinkles around his eyes deepened.

"Thanks. I needed some quiet time." Connor fiddled with the watch on his left hand.

"I understand. The chapel is definitely the place for quiet reflection." The minister gazed at him. He seemed unhurried. Connor decided a minister would be the right person for unburdening.

"I'm confused. I may have alienated the one person that meant the most to me. She's a pretty forgiving person, but I don't know…"

"You have a loved one in hospital?"

"My daughter, Christie."

The silence extended for a few seconds before Connor spoke again.

"The trouble started a few days ago. My girlfriend, Gypsy, believed that Christie had been poisoned. I didn't believe her, I told her she was crazy and stormed out earlier today. I got myself a room in a local hotel. I found out a few minutes ago that Gypsy was right my daughter has been poisoned. They've given her the antidote, but it's still touch and go."

"I see." The minister gazed at Connor.

"The trouble is really about another issue. You see, many years ago, Christie's mother and I had an affair. Christie was born nine months later. My brother and sister-in-law died when Christie and her brother were young and we took them both in. I've never spoken to Christie about my suspicions that I was her biological father, I've been too afraid. The paternity results came back a while ago. Positive."

"I understand," murmured the minister.

"I'm so confused. I don't know what to do. Obviously, now isn't the time to talk to Christie, but I'm afraid I've pushed Gypsy away so far she'll never speak to me again. My loyalty should have been to her, but I let fear take over. I just hope she'll forgive me."

"If she is the woman you say she is, I'm sure things will work out," said the minister, his hands resting lightly on his lap.

"I'm not so sure. I don't know what to think." Connor gazed at one of the stained glass windows, his mouth turned down.

"At times like this, myself, I usually pray. Would you mind if I pray for you?"

"I guess," Connor said. At this moment, the soothing tones of a minister praying for him couldn't hurt.

He bowed his head and listened to the lullaby that was the minister softly praying for his peace and tranquility and for Christie's health.

As the minister's head came up, Connor thanked him and got up from the pew to head back to the hospital corridor to wait for more news.

On the way, he summoned up the courage to send a text to Gypsy. That way he'd know whether she was willing to talk to him.

He swiped at his phone and tapped out a message:

I'm so sorry. I never should have doubted you. You were right Christie was poisoned. She is in intensive care now. Let me know if you're willing to talk.

He slapped his telephone shut and quickened his pace down the hospital corridor to resume the vigil with Ryan.

***

Tuesday 22nd January, 7.38pm

Ryan retrieved his phone, which had been buzzing all day, and switched it to silent mode. He really didn't want to talk to anyone. However, he decided he'd check his text messages while he waited for news about Christie's condition.

There was one from the security company that managed the silent alarm at their property. *Alarm activation 7.26am today. Please call immediately.*

As he put the phone to his ear, and walked toward the main entrance, he remembered Gypsy's claim the day before—that Brenton had poisoned Christie in a twisted bid to start a relationship with him. He still struggled with it all.

"Stellar Security."

"Yes, I've just had a message that the alarm at my property was activated."

The woman who answered the phone took his name and he gave them the code agreed upon to verify his identity.

"Yes, sir, we've been attempting to contact you all day. Would you like us to report the matter to police?"

"No, but thank you. I haven't been home for a while—I have a family member in hospital. I might just check to see if everything's okay."

"We do usually recommend you inform the police department, sir."

"I am a member of the police force."

The woman paused. "I see. In that case, please let me know if there is anything we can do to assist."

Once she hung up, Ryan began a slow jog toward his car.

If Brenton had actually broken into their home, all hell would break loose. He wanted to beat the living shit out of him. He'd tried to kill his girl. He'd broken into his house. The guy had a problem, and needed a wake-up call. Ryan wanted to punch him repeatedly until he got the message. He ground his teeth and tightened his hands on the steering wheel. As he ducked and weaved through traffic, he tried to remember the car parked outside his home, a white smallish car, Japanese make.

As he pulled into the driveway, he searched for the car and couldn't see it. Didn't mean Brenton wasn't here, though.

He retrieved a bunch of keys from his pocket and unlocked the door. As he pushed it open, he saw two men on the floor of his lounge room. Brenton he recognized immediately, the dirty weasel, and the other man with him seemed familiar—from the bar, Jake. Brenton was in tears and Jake was beside him with one hand on his shoulder.

Clenching his fists, Ryan stormed toward them.

***

Tuesday 22nd January, 8.22pm

My phone beeped. I lay across the couch, thinking about Connor, wondering if and when we'd ever salvage our relationship. I picked up my mobile phone and there it was, the message I'd been hoping for.

I smiled slowly and sagged back in the couch. I let out a huge breath. Finally. I typed back a message to Connor.

I'm so glad. How is Christie?

Knowing Connor, he'd respond quickly.

Within less than a minute, my telephone pinged at me again.

Thank you. I can't tell you how sorry I am. I was worried you'd never speak to me again. Doc says they gave her the antidote a few hours ago, just in time. You saved her life.

Hot tears blazed down my cheeks. I hadn't expected thanks, but when it came, the acknowledgement from the one that mattered most left me shaking with relief.

With trembling hands, I tapped out a reply. *Should I come to the hospital, or do you need time alone?*

I'd love to see you. Are you at home?

Yes, I replied.

I'll be there soon.

I jumped up from the couch and ran for the bathroom, where I checked my reflection. I was wearing an old tracksuit, my hair looked like it had seen better days, and I had not a trace of make-up on my face. I quickly searched for an outfit, choosing a pair of black pants and a cream top. I dragged a brush through my hair and swiped on some lip-gloss, enough to satisfy for the moment.

Scanning the apartment—yikes!—I began to tidy up, removing items from the floor, throwing dirty clothing in the laundry, and frantically unpacking and repacking the dishwasher.

I heard a key turn in the lock of the front door.

"Connor." I spoke quietly, but he heard me. I broke into a run. When I reached Connor, I threw my arms around him. I whispered in his ear, "You don't get rid of me that easily."

He pulled me away to look at me with wet eyes and a watery smile. Then he bent his head again and kissed me, tentative and soft.

"I can't tell you how sorry I am," he said and held me. "Thank you for talking to me."

"I'm glad you called."

"Come with me." Connor took my hand and gently, unsure at first, led me upstairs. I followed him in silence. He closed the door of the bedroom behind us and began to undress me, slowly and carefully, his eyes never leaving mine.

Once he had taken in my presence, his eyes moved to rake over me, taking in every inch. The scene seemed almost surreal, just minutes ago we'd been apart, now, here he was, gorgeous, loving, and attentive. My body tingled, aching to be with him again. He stepped forward to take me in his arms. Gently, Connor pulled me onto the bed and his mouth melted into mine, carefully at first, as warmth spread across my body. As I returned it, Connor deepened the kiss, his arms moving across my back and up to caress my neck.

All I was aware of was Connor touching every expanse of my body. For the first in a long time, I forgot everything else—all of the problems, the heartache, the worry. There was only Connor and I.

Ecstasy sent shivers through my body, and I teetered on the edge of bliss. It was as if my skin had become something else, hypersensitive to the slightest touch. My hands caressed his smooth shoulder blades until he sighed. Then I moved down, searching for the next spot that would cause him to melt. I explored the curve of his spine and buttocks while my lips opened to his. My lips opened and the electric sensation of our tongues encircling sent such a spark of delicious shock through my body that Connor stopped, lifted his head, and smiled at me.

I smiled and curled my arms around his neck, drawing him back to me. Suddenly I couldn't rein in my urges any longer. I took his hand and placed it between my legs. He lifted his head so that his tongue and mine could merge, and his fingers began to caress the moistness, gently at first, then firmer. I moaned, and beneath it, I heard a low rumble that was Connor's growl. I wrapped a leg around him and felt him tight against me, the pulse of him blazing and needy.

And suddenly Connor was above me. His lips kissed my cheeks, my nose, my eyes, until I opened them and found him looking down on me with an expression so filled with love that I knew I would carry it with me for a long time to come.

"Gypsy," he breathed. "I'm so sorry. I'll never leave you again. Ever. Tell me this is what you want."

In reply, I bucked my hips so that the tip of him slid inside me. Connor gasped. With infinite care, he entered me and he held me close, murmuring and whispering. "I love you Gypsy, I always have and I always will. No matter what."

We moved together, slowly at first, then building until the room shattered into dozens of shards of light. Connor called out, holding on to me tightly, a sheen of sweat across his back.

As we lay on the bed, breathing deeply, the room came back into focus. I saw that Connor's eyes were hooded, but a smile lit his face.

His arms were around me, and he kissed me again, on the forehead, the nose, the mouth.

"I love you," he said. In that moment I was the happiest I'd been in a long time.

As I lay in the afterglow, my thoughts turned to Christie and Ryan. I hoped they'd be okay. If Isabella had anything to do with it, they would be. I played our last conversation back in my mind, and sucked in a sharp breath. Would Brenton really break into their home? Is that what she said?

It was some time before I could speak. Not meaning to alarm Connor, I asked him about his daughter and where Ryan was. Connor seemed hopeful that Christie would recover, but there'd been no sign of Ryan for a while.

"Actually, I messaged him with no reply," he said.

In that moment, I had a suspicion of where Ryan had gone. *It was time to move, and fast.*

"Does he have an alarm system at home?"

"Yes, a silent alarm."

"We have to get to Ryan and Christie's. Isabella mentioned in passing that Brenton might break into their home. It seemed crazy at the time, but now I'm not so sure. If Ryan learned the alarm went off, he's probably on his way there. How long has he been gone?"

"I'm not sure, maybe an hour or two, possibly longer?"

I grabbed Connor's hand. "We need to get dressed and get going, *now*. Once Ryan gets hold of Brenton …"

At record speed, we showered and dressed, then sped toward the doors, and broke into a run for our cars.

Gypsy Cradle

***

CHAPTER 15

Chapter Fifteen

Tuesday 22nd January, 8.23pm

Ryan's vision clouded as his heart pounded in his ears. He moved slowly and deliberately toward Brenton. The bastard that almost killed Christie slumped on their couch. *Our couch. Fuck.* He wanted blood. With a guttural roar, Ryan stormed toward him.

"You fucking bastard. You poisoned Christie!"

Jake stepped in front of Ryan, palms up in an effort to calm him. "Hang on. You don't understand–"

Ryan jabbed a finger in Jake's face. "I don't *understand*? Did you know about this?"

Jake stuttered. "Ah, ah–"

"Answer me!" Ryan screamed. "I'll punch your fucking head in too."

Jake blinked, his gaze ping ponging. "I didn't until a couple of minutes ago. He was going to turn himself in right after I called the hospital. But busting his face won't help."

"It'll help me, you stupid bastard! The only reason she's still alive is because of her sister-in-law. She knows about what he did. I hope they lock the piece of shit up forever." Ryan moved his gaze to target Brenton but Brenton wouldn't meet his eyes. He had curled up on the couch.

"You're angry," Jake said. "I don't blame you, but let's calm down."

"Calm down? Are you fucking serious?" Ryan let out a hard, brittle laugh. "My girlfriend nearly died. Get out of my way." Jake shoved him, hard. He landed on the floor, arms and legs sprawled, and Ryan lunged for Brenton.

As Ryan grabbed him by the collar and lifted his body from the couch, Brenton let out a piercing scream.

"Please, no, you don't understand. No!" He flinched.

Ryan pulled back a fist and it connected with Brenton's nose with a sickening crunch of bone and blood. Brenton reached up blindly, his nails connecting with Ryan's neck. He drew blood. Engulfed in rage, the smell of blood seemed to spur Ryan on. He pulled his fist back and punched

Brenton again and again, the force of each impact doing more damage.

Jake pushed himself up from the floor and lunged for Ryan, attempting to separate them. "What are you doing? You're killing him!"

"You mess with my girl, you mess with me," Ryan hissed through gritted teeth. He pulled his fist back, ready for a final blow. Jake grabbed at Ryan's arm from behind, attempting to hold him back, but he didn't have the strength to match him.

Jake, still holding on, watched in horror as Ryan's fist connected with Brenton's eye socket for a second time. With a howl, Brenton attempted to wriggle away, the beginnings of a bruise searing across his eye socket. "What is wrong with you?" yelled Jake, holding Brenton's face between his hands to survey the damage.

"What's wrong with *me*? I haven't tried to kill anyone. Yet." Ryan clenched and unclenched his fists.

"Let's get out of here!" Jake grabbed at Brenton's shirt, dragging him toward the front door just a few feet away.

"You don't get off that easy," growled Ryan, stomping after them. He grasped at Jake, who twisted around to face him.

"Do you really want to kill him?" Jake struggled to catch his breath, shoulders heaving. "Then what?"

Ryan sucked in a ragged breath, glaring at the two pathetic figures. Jake had Brenton by the shirtsleeve. Brenton stooped over, clutching one hand over his nose in a vain attempt to contain the blood dripping from it. It dribbled through his fingers, and his eye was almost swollen shut. His hand muffled the sobbing.

In that instant, Ryan realized he could lose everything over this. He knew Brenton's type—a victim mentality. He'd drive straight from here to the cop shop to lodge a formal complaint. But Ryan's career and his life were worth more than that. As Ryan watched Brenton and Jake hobble through the front door, their pitiful figures seemed inconsequential, unimportant considering he had risked so much to take his revenge.

"I'd already talked him into ringing the hospital to confess and save her life. Killing him won't fix this." Jake's pallid face almost glowed. He scrutinized Ryan and waited for a response.

None came.

Jake pushed Brenton the last few feet to the front door. "Get out!"

Brenton went first, levering the front door open with a forearm as his hand was cupped over his nose. They shuffled toward the car.

As the screen door slammed behind them, Ryan headed for an armchair.

***

Tuesday 22nd January, 8.24pm

Connor and I ran to our cars.

"Meet you there!" I yelled. I figured he'd get there faster than I would, especially in an unmarked cop car with a siren.

It took forever to unlock the damn car. My hands were shaking so badly I struggled to open the thing; then the battery on my digital car lock was flat and of course, in the quiet that was eleven months of seemingly peaceful existence who would have thought I'd need to change the battery to cope with an emergency like this?

I opened the door and swung my body in, landing hard on the driver's seat. I shoved the key into the ignition and took a second to compose myself. I shook the stress out of my hands and breathed deeply, attempting to orient myself and gain some sense of calm. I was kidding myself—my fingers trembled so hard I struggled to keep hold of the steering wheel.

Slamming the door closed, I took off, steering the car out of the driveway. How would I react if Ryan *had* killed Brenton? A picture of bodies pushed its way in. Bodies battered and bleeding were strewn across their lounge room floor with dark red sprays decorating the walls.

I pushed the image away fast. I needed calm, not imaginary pictures of a worst-case scenario. I pushed hard against the persistent horrific image until it left for good. I breathed out. The rush of relief at being back in the fold of Connor's love had dimmed after learning of the crisis with Ryan. The last thing we needed now was another crisis, a crime of passion involving Ryan and Brenton. I just hoped we'd get there in time.

I'd been lost in the past for too long and so had Connor. Right now, we needed to handle the hell out of the here and now.

The terror surging through my veins sprung from the unknown, and in the face of the unknown, my mind conjured up the wildest scenes possible. I knew Connor would be there with me. That might not prepare me for the sight of bleeding, broken bodies strewn across a living room floor though. I'd been lucky, I hadn't seen many corpses and I damn well didn't want to see the general gruesomeness that would result if Ryan had beaten the crap out of Brenton. Or did I? I'd surprised myself with my taste for vengeance when I'd held Aaron captive. No way in hell, I'd be going there again. There was too much at stake.

When Aaron had almost killed me in the hit and run, I'd discovered a new very handy skill. It had saved my life once already. I'd been able to track Aaron down telepathically by sifting through signature visions or pictures to see the memory of the kidnapping I'd interrupted. I'd found him and discovered his plan to break into my house and torture me. So I damn well tortured him back. I'd considered doing the same to Brenton after all the crap I'd been through. Considered, but I'd learned my lesson. It was one thing to crave something, another to put plans into action. Plus I hadn't been able to find Brenton over the last couple of days, which seemed to be a blessing in disguise.

Of course, if I had found Brenton, I might have made him pay before turning him in to the cops. Wouldn't work this time though, we'd have to sort this one out the regular way.

I drove like a demon, hoping I would get there in short order, although it was at best a fifteen minute journey. Thankfully, it was daytime traffic, but I still cursed and screamed at other drivers to get out of my damn way—didn't they understand the emergency?

Adrenaline coursed through me, exhaustion a thing of the past. I needed to power on. I drove at full capacity, and tried not to think about the gauge showing I was slightly over the speed limit, a consequence of having a cop for a boyfriend.

As I swerved around cars that were turning right, I cursed them. I deliberately focused on the present, banishing all thoughts other than what desperately needed to be done. It worked. I pulled to a stop outside Ryan and Christie's place. Connor's car was already parked outside. I slammed the car door shut and locked it, before I peered around their home, at the driveway, the garden, the windows, one of which had been left open. The place looked surprisingly quiet. No other cars around. No signs of screaming, fighting, blood, gore or drama.

I found the front door open. Ryan sat slumped against the wall of the hallway, head in his hands.

Connor crouched beside him. Neither of them registered my arrival.

"We need to call it in." Connor's deep, quiet voice sounded somber.

Ryan didn't respond. His fingers laced his hair, and what I could see of his face looked ashen. This different Ryan disconcerted me, his usual confidence a thing of the past. The shaking, shambolic figure with head down appeared confused, unsure, and not the assured person I'd known.

Then, he might have just killed a man. If he had, I shuddered to think of the impact this would have on the shell of a man before me, as well as his girlfriend and possible future father to be.

"I didn't kill him. He was alive when he left," Ryan mumbled, answering my unasked question.

I stood fixed to the floor a few feet away, behind the carpet trim separating the tiled hallway from the living area, and watched events unfold in silence.

Connor said, "I'll call it in, then we'll work it out. Break and enter, attempted murder, this is serious stuff. Let the experts help."

He extended a hand to Ryan and lifted him from the cold tiled floor. As Ryan stood, he stumbled on shaky legs. He regarded me blankly before acknowledging my presence with the trace of a nod.

He fell into an armchair with his limbs hanging over the sides. He looked exhausted—had he worn himself out beating Brenton to death? The scumbag deserved it, but Connor couldn't stand to have another family member in jail. He headed for the same corner, lips moving slowly as he murmured into the phone.

I stood unmoving as he passed me. My heart pounded as I saw speckles of blood on the tiles. The scene reminded me far too much of my run in with Aaron almost a year ago. I flicked a glance at Ryan hoping he would speak. As I padded toward a chair in the opposite corner and perched on the edge of my seat, his voice broke. I wondered if my thoughts about whether he'd murdered a man had anything to do with the timing of his speech.

"I didn't kill him, but I wanted to. I reckon I broke his nose and smashed his eye," He brought his arms up to cross them.

My lips moved without words, a fish out of water. Eventually my voice box connected with my mind and the words came. "When did they leave?"

"Ten minutes ago." Ryan left his chair, heading for the bathroom, probably to clean the dried blood from his hands.

Connor finished his official business and shoved his phone into a pocket. "They'll be here soon."

"What happens now?" I said, rubbing my chin.

"They'll take a statement. If they consider Ryan used excessive force, they'll take it further, talking to his senior. Highly unlikely, though. Then they'll find Brenton and charge him."

Ryan arrived back with chin high, seemingly a changed man. "Christie, she'll be okay, I'm sure of it but if she wakes up..."

"It's okay, mate, remember what the doctor said. Any news and they'll call straight away," said Connor.

Ryan's feet were wide apart, his arms crossed. "I beat the crap out of him and I'm glad. He's lucky to be alive..."

I regarded Connor, wishing I could crawl into his head and get a sense of what he felt. I'd tried to get a handle on Brenton with my telepathic signature ability. I hoped to hell Connor hadn't got in the way. At times, I suffered sneaking suspicions that Connor barred me from learning what he was *really* feeling, still not completely comfortable with what I could do. Damn sentinels.

He approached Ryan, speaking in a low, soothing voice. "I get it, I do. It can get to us…The Mr. Stinky case has been rough. But you're not alone. It's over now. Christie will be fine. We can put this behind us."

The Mr. Stinky case? I wondered if that name had been given to the ongoing serial assault investigation Connor had mentioned briefly. He didn't like to bring work home, so when he did, I knew it meant a disturbing case had got to him, one that pushed the boundaries. It had taken eighteen months before they caught the criminal. Ryan must have been hunting him, too.

Ryan raised an eyebrow. "It'll come up once they get here. Excessive force. Then an interview with the senior sergeant and maybe a board hearing—the last thing I need."

Connor stood directly across from Ryan, the light casting shadows across his handsome face. God. "It won't get that far. Brenton drew blood. Surely you saw the scratch in the mirror?"

Ryan gave Connor the thumbs-up signal.

Connor continued, "I've been there. It builds up, and creeps like him get under your skin. Especially when they threaten family." He clapped a hand on Ryan's shoulder. "We've got this. I'm on your side."

Ryan shook his head. "I let it get to me. I've been a prick. To Christie, to you and Gypsy." Ryan levered his body around before swinging back. "A tough case is no excuse. I'm sorry."

"Don't worry, we'll sort it out," Connor said, the timbre of his voice reassuring and deep.

I damn well hoped so.

***

Tuesday 22nd January, 8.29pm

Drips and spatters of blood had dried on Brenton's face, and tears had added to the mess. After Ryan threatened him, insisting he shut the hell up, the hysterical screams had been suppressed into muffled whimpers. His nose sat at a frightening angle, and his left eye was bruised and battered. He limped for the car with Jake following closely behind.

"I'm dying," he panted, dried and fresh blood mingling with dirt from his hands where he had wiped his face repeatedly.

"Shut up," puffed Jake. "Need to get to hospital."

Neither of them uttered a word until they reached the car. Hunched over and gasping, they fell against the driver's side door. Jake spoke first.

"No. You're not driving. *Ridiculous*," he said. "I'm not going to jail. Let me get my stuff." Brenton lunged for the boot, but Jake barred his way.

"Brenton!" Jake ripped his hand away from the car lock. He reached for Brenton's shaking right forearm where he had almost connected the key with the lock. Jake grabbed at his shoulder, pushing his hand down onto Brenton's arm in a vain attempt to wrestle him for the keys to open the driver's side door. He used his hip and shoulder to push Brenton aside.

"Fuck off, Jake!" Brenton pushed back.

"Fuck off? After everything I've done, all I've been through, that's all you have?" Jake's face was crimson. The blood flowing from Brenton's nose had slowed to a drip. The trail became smaller as it led from the front door down the driveway to the bitumen.

They eyed each other. Initially, the suburban street had been empty, thankfully without witnesses. Their good luck couldn't last. A screen door slammed and a middle-aged woman emerged, stepping carefully down the front steps, walking across her garden to stand at the curb on the other side of the road, with hands on hips, eagle-eyed as events unfolded.

"Get in the fucking car. *Now*!" Brenton's voice reached fever pitch. He yelled at full volume again and Jake relented. The bystander took a step closer. Jake stomped over to the passenger door and wrenched on the door handle. It wouldn't open.

"Are you going to unlock it, then?" he demanded of Brenton. Through the window, he could see his friend struggling to open the locked car with trembling fingers.

"Hurry up!" roared Jake. He patted his pockets, feeling for the bulk of his telephone. The entire situation had escalated way past the point where he previously estimated he would be in control. Previously he'd been able to restrain Brenton's nervous hysteria, but something, or rather someone, had taken hold of his friend in a way that terrified him. If he could get the authorities here, the mess could be nipped in the bud early, before Brenton did something stupid, like jump off a bridge. He knew now, with horrifying certainty, that he had underestimated him.

Time to call an ambulance. The mobile however, had gone missing in action.

The car bounced as Brenton threw his battered body into the car seat. He shoved the key into the ignition and leaned over to unlock Jake's side of the car. The passenger door swung open with considerable force.

"Drive!" roared Jake, slamming it shut.

Brenton took off, revving the vehicle, almost past its capabilities. The windscreen wipers started up despite there being no trace of rain. The car lurched forward violently until it skidded to a stop. Brenton had stalled it.

"Drive, drive, go, go, *go*!" Jake, rubbed his face with his hands.

He couldn't look. The fact that Brenton wouldn't answer his question, combined with a sense of impending doom, meant he struggled with the reality of what they faced. Sure, he'd got Brenton out of scrapes before, but this was different. He struggled to drag Brenton out of the alternating hysteria and terror, tinged with a sense of apathy, accepting his fate, whatever that may be. Jake wasn't sure if he wanted to be a part of it anymore.

Tears dripped from Brenton's mangled eye sockets. "Shut up, shut up, I'm trying!"

He started the car up again, jamming his foot down on the accelerator more than needed. They drove for a minute without speaking.

"To the hospital," Jake said.

"No!"

"Well, let me fucking drive!"

"No," cried Brenton, "*No!*"

"Do you want to die? Do you?"

Brenton didn't answer.

A flurry of red fur flashed in front of the car's grille. Brenton jammed on the brakes and the car skidded, but not in time to escape the sickening scrape of the car's wheel arches along planters lining the nature strip. Before they had time to cry out, a young woman with long blonde hair sprinted after the dog.

Brenton swung the steering wheel for hard left. Jake threw his hands out in a grab for it, but too late. It had already locked up. Brenton screamed. The small russet cocker spaniel pup and his round-eyed owner made it to safety as the car careened toward a gray power pole.

***

Tuesday 22nd January, 8.31pm

The bell rang. Connor sprung up and bounded over to answer it. Two men in navy blue uniforms had pulled open the squeaking screen door. The blond male constable flashed a badge, gestured to his colleague, and disappeared. His dark-haired colleague stepped over the threshold.

I'd been here before, eleven months ago. I had some idea of how this rolled out. The uniformed cop entered the living area, and ducked through the archway.

"Martin" The constable folded his frame onto the couch. Connor remained standing, rubbing the back of his neck. I sat in the chair further down the room in an attempt to remain a fly on the wall. I wondered if I'd be asked to leave.

"So tell me about this break and enter." The statement from our dark-haired friend, who I saw from his nametag was Constable Jones, carried a hint of cynicism.

"Yeah," muttered Ryan, sitting on the arm of a chair at the edge of the lounge room.

"Can you run us through it?" A large notepad appeared on Constable Jones' knee.

"Well, er, Christie, my girlfriend, is in intensive care. Touch and go." He gestured with one hand, a man with a whole lot to worry about, and answers coming too slowly. "I got a text from the alarm company while I was at the hospital–"

"How long ago was this?"

"I don't know, maybe an hour ago."

"Okay. Carry on."

"When I got here, I found Jake and the perpetrator in the lounge room and…"

I saw a solid, black mass of silence fill the room. The outcome of this could mean the difference between a career continuing or ending. Obviously, the two uniformed officers knew that, and it looked like they had their own history, judging by the black mass sitting in between them. Not that they'd let on to either Ryan or Connor, but I could see it.

The officers were keeping secrets, and Ryan didn't want to tell them he'd beaten the crap out of Jake and Brenton, or that one of them had poisoned Christie. How would he explain his knowledge of such a crisis? A thirst for revenge? That a psychic had helped identify the bad guy? Did Ryan know that Connor was a sentinel? I didn't think so, but I couldn't be sure. My mouth went dry. The urge to run from the room surged within me, and I pushed it back down. I wanted to run, run as fast as I could to the safety and sanctity of my home. I pressed my hands deeper into the arms of the chair.

What had I done? Maybe if I'd kept my visits from Isabella to myself, none of us would be here in this room, at this time. For the same reason, if I had kept quiet, maybe Christie would no longer be with us. Regardless, I'd charged ahead like a bull at a gate, reckless, impulsive. Concepts of integrity and honor, so vital days ago, seemed silly, self-indulgent in the face of such a heavily charged atmosphere. My spontaneous behavior could lead to me being outed in a cringe-worthy episode involving four police, in a so far serious interview. One where more remained unspoken than said directly.

Oh god.

"The perpetrators are known to you?" asked Constable Jones, writing in his notepad.

He seemed unduly formal considering the black mass I'd detected earlier , but he probably did so due to the presence of a civilian, not wanting to let on that they'd both been tempted to take matters into their own hands at times,—not that I'd been introduced, or planned to be for that matter.

"Um, yes." Ryan didn't elaborate. The skin around his eyes had bunched up, a muscle under his cheek twitching.

"You know them how?" Constable Jones' pencil hung poised over the notepad.

Connor broke his silence. "Can we go into more detail at the station later tonight? Ryan isn't in any state to answer anything now. His girlfriend's in ICU." I heard the tremor in his voice and wondered if Jones noticed it, if it would make him suspicious.

"I understand that. But the best time to go over this is right now while it's fresh in his mind, as I'm sure you're aware, Detective Reardon."

Right.

Ryan rubbed his hands down his jeans. "I met Jake and Brenton at a bar Saturday night. I'd had a few. Unwinding after the Mr. Stinky case. I didn't realize Brenton works with Christie—she's my girlfriend, Connor's niece."

I watched the caster wheels on Ryan's chair roll an inch back and forth.

Constable Jones continued to scrutinize Ryan, who wasn't in a hurry to answer anything.

"He broke into your home for what reason? Why would he want to break in? The doors and windows were secured?"

I exchanged glances with Connor, wondering why in the hell the cop seemed so antagonistic to Ryan. Surely the boys in blue stuck together, looked out for each other? What was going on here?

Connor acknowledged me with a barely perceptible nod.

"I don't know," Ryan was saying. "Guilty conscience maybe. From what I've been told, the guy is twisted, a bit of a sicko, a stalker type. I haven't been with it the last few days, but I'm not surprised. All I care about right now is Christie. If anything happens and I lose her…" His voice cracked, and he wrung his hands. In that moment, I wanted to rush over and comfort him, despite his antagonistic treatment of me previously.

Connor took a step closer. His prior edginess had been replaced with an air of tranquility. He thrived on crisis; when the chips were down and it all hit the fan, my man seemed to descend into a cloud of calm.

Constable Jones raised a hand. "I understand that. We need to get to the bottom of this. Why do you say he's a stalker type? Ryan?"

Ryan's cheeks blazed. "I drank too much Saturday night. A case got to me; I know it shouldn't but...Christie and I had a bit of a row and I stormed off. I had a few too many, and a couple of blokes helped me home."

I noticed he skipped the part about waking up naked in their home, but then, it wasn't exactly polite conversation.

Constable Jones cocked an eyebrow "The perpetrators?"

"Yeah," Ryan mumbled.

"And they broke into your home? Why?" Officer Jones raised an eyebrow and scowled.

I hoped Ryan wouldn't answer the question and help Jones join the dots.

"God knows why, he's nuts. I found him and his mate Jake in my lounge room today. I screamed at them to leave, and hurt one of them, before they ran out of here."

"I see," said Constable Jones, his brow wrinkled. "Do you know their surnames? Or address, by any chance?"

"Er, no," Ryan said, looking away.

The screen door banged closed and the blond haired uniform walked in.

"Neighbor got a registration plate. White Corolla?"

Constable Jones peered at Ryan.

"I think so," he said.

The blond uniform entered to stand on the other side of Ryan. He had moved close enough that I could see his name badge: Constable Williams. "Mrs. Briggs saw them fighting before they got in the car and took off. One of them was bleeding from the face."

"Good, we'll track them down with the rego plate. How many times did you punch him?" Constable Jones closed the notebook and tucked his pen in the pocket of his shirt.

"I don't remember saying I punched him." Ryan shifted his weight from one foot to the other. "But I did injure him, yes."

"Okay." Constable Williams got up from the chair, which creaked as it stood. "Leave it with us. Doesn't sound like excessive force to me, but I'll need to take a statement from this Brenton character."

Connor loitered, edging closer to Ryan, who spoke looking at the floor. "Yeah, okay."

"I might have to speak to your boss, if it's warranted."

"Yeah, I know how it goes."

Constable Williams flicked his chin upwards, and Constable Jones' heels clicked on the tiled hallway floor. Ryan shook his hand. Connor did the same, while I hung back, conscious of the boys' club meeting. My name hadn't come up once, which could only be a good thing.

With authority reflecting from their lapels, the officers walked back through the archway, shoulders rounded, more than likely knowing they'd get no more information from Ryan, and then Connor and Ryan followed. Their deep voices rumbled down the hall and the door slammed closed.

Ryan returned to the room and sighed. "Thank god that's over. I'm going back to the hospital to see how Christie's doing."

"Yeah," said Connor, checking his mobile phone. "Oh my god." He smiled slowly and sagged back against the wall. "Christie's regained consciousness."

"Say that again," Ryan, rubbed battered looking fingers through his hair.

"She's okay. Christie's okay. The hospital probably messaged you, too."

"I'm going in." Ryan shuffled his keys in his pocket.

"You heard what the doctor said. We need rest first. Let's get some sleep, and we'll meet there in the morning," Connor said. Sounded like he wanted to talk to me, in private, judging by the knowing glance cast in my direction before Ryan left. Maybe he knew something I didn't, which would make a nice change.

***

Tuesday 22nd January, 8.51pm

The small white car slammed into the pole with a stomach-turning crunch. Then silence, other than the hiss of a radiator. The white car's grille had missed the girl by inches. She dragged her phone from a pocket, pressing it to her ear with a ripple of quaking fingers.

She peered into the car and began to weep. One man's forehead was lodged in the windscreen, a star of blood radiating from the shattered glass. The other man mumbled incoherently with not a mark on him. His seatbelt, locked in place, had saved his life.

She hung up, despite the operator's advice to her to watch and wait, and attempted to open the badly dented passenger door. She squatted by the window, attempting with hand signals and facial expressions to calm Jake. The puppy had darted up the street before stopping at the edge of the busy road. Two men and a woman emerged from the driveway of a home meters up the street. She waited for the ambulance.

***

CHAPTER 16

Chapter Sixteen

Tuesday 22nd January, 9.02pm

The homes along Lineside Way, Brunswick were lit up like Christmas trees, the blue whirring light of the ambulance shining a beacon that drew crowds. Women in aprons crossed their arms, peering down the street, seeking titillation. Of course, the paramedics wouldn't give anything away, but Mary Briggs at number seventeen knew what it was all about. She whispered in her closest neighbor Ray's ear that it would have been something to do with the two hooligans she saw arguing earlier. She puffed out her chest as she explained confidently that the police had interviewed her. She couldn't stress enough the importance of paying attention to one's environment. Luckily, that nice police officer lived further up the street, and they'd come out to see what caused the horrible bang. Oh, how that handsome blond police officer's ears had pricked up when she'd passed on what she saw.

They'd crashed just a few hundred meters down the road. At first, it sounded like a gunshot. She'd wandered down the road in her slippers and discovered that poor young girl, practically hysterical. Irresponsible drivers. One of them looked dirty, with dried blood caked all over his face and the start of a black eye taking shape. Before they got in the car, he wouldn't stop screaming at his friend who sounded like he just wanted to help. The whole nasty business shocked her. Nothing like this ever happened in Brunswick. Mainly families and busy young couples minded their own business in this neighborhood.

Mary elbowed Ray as the ambulance stretcher clicked onto the rail in the back of the emergency vehicle and the paramedic slid one man into the back of the ambulance. She knew he was conscious, she'd heard him moan. As for the other one with the mangled face, she had no idea. He hadn't moved or made a sound.

"That's him," she said before her lips pressed together...

"Um…who?" Ray asked, fumbling with his watch.

"The passenger. Tried to tell that idiot he shouldn't drive with his eye puffed up like that but he wouldn't listen. He could have killed someone."

Ray's mouth formed an O. He shuffled his feet and gazed longingly through a window to the flickering TV inside. The first cricket test scores were close it might be a tie. The game would be over soon.

The second paramedic slammed the back doors closed and swung into the driver's cabin with her partner. The siren blasted a few short pips before the vehicle started down the hill. A little boy ran down the hill, smiling in his attempts to beat it.

Ray grabbed his walking stick and hobbled in to check on the cricket scores. Mary stayed to ensure everyone knew what was going on before treading inside to catch the news.

****

Tuesday 22nd January, 9.04pm

Connor froze in place. Sure, he'd used his ability for the first time he could remember to block Isabella from communicating with Gypsy any further.

However, this, this was different. It could change everything.

He'd blocked an attempt, a communication Isabella initiated with Gypsy. One that contained bad news, news he could never, ever pass on to Gypsy. It showed foresight, planning, and intent. Which left him wondering about Isabella's motives?

Surely, as a child, she wasn't capable of something like this. He struggled with the implications of it all.

"Don't go out there just yet. Give it a minute or two."

Gypsy swiped the hair from her eyes, and shuffled, impatient to get away.

"What? Why not?"

"Something's happened."

"What do you mean something's happened? What are you talking about?"

"It's Isabella. She just tried to get in touch with you. I intercepted the transmission, for wont of a better word."

"You did?" If he thought Gypsy was impatient earlier, judging by the folded arms and the biting of a lip, she bordered on anxiety now. "Wow, I thought all that telepathic stuff was my domain. So you had a second crack at flexing your sentinel muscles, hey?" Her face wore that cheeky expression he knew and loved so well. "What did she say?"

It wasn't what she said that was the problem, but what she did.

"There's been a car accident, just a few hundred meters from here."

"Oh my god let me see, Connor, let me out there."

He placed one hand gently on her back, and brought her closer to him. Her warm, soft figure sent a rush of warmth through him, reinforcing the instinct to protect.

"She told me about the accident. Brenton and Jake. It's serious."

Gypsy stared up at him, mouth open.

"An accident? How serious? In what way?"

"Well, she knew about it. I didn't want to pass on the bad news."

"Bad news, hell, the fact that Brenton is out of the way is good news, isn't it? Although his friend Jake doesn't deserve this, he sure as hell does. Karma's a bitch."

Gypsy pushed the screen door open and headed toward the street. A frown dominated Ryan's face, and his attention was riveted on ambulance officers outside a car, which had hit a power pole.

A crowd gathered on the other side of the street.

Connor touched Ryan's shoulder. "Come away mate. Let's go home for now. Things will be better in the morning"

Shaking himself out of his reverie, Ryan turned his head and seemed to come back to the present. "I recognize the car. That's dickhead, isn't it? Brenton & Co."

Connor didn't answer.

Gypsy elbowed him. "So what's the go then? Are you going to give me the inside skinny then or what? You have an exclusive relationship with Isabella all of a sudden, do you?" Her smile, initially a parting of the lips, gave way to a fully-fledged toothy grin. He smiled in spite of himself.

"We'll see." He said, and gestured toward their cars. "Let's get to the hospital and we'll see."

As they walked slowly toward the cars, he breathed a sigh of relief. He hadn't needed to tell her that Isabella had somehow excited the puppy, enough that it suddenly bolted in front of the car. She had planned the whole thing. So much for her childlike demeanor, she had a vengeful streak a mile long. If his suspicions panned out the way he expected, they were in for more surprises yet.

The last thing they needed was another impulsive, stubborn, fiercely loyal psychic interfering in family matters.

He figured he probably didn't have any choice in the matter, as he rarely did once Gypsy decided on a reckless course of action. He unlocked the car door, and nodded to Ryan as they got into the cars.

He'd hold onto his secret as long as he had to. The responsibilities of a sentinel were becoming clear to him, far too clear for his liking.

***

Wednesday 23rd January, 9.04am

Jake raised his bandaged head a few inches from the pillow before letting it fall back. A hammer pounded in his right temple. His left leg wouldn't move. Tearing the sheet away, he peered down at the limb. A black and grey moon boot meant he wouldn't be going anyway in a hurry.

The crash couldn't have happened at a worse time. Hot tears gathered in the corners of Jake's eyes. Yes, the dog jumped in front of their car, but if he'd insisted harder, been more persistent, he could have driven them both to safety. He should never have let Brenton drive, particularly at that time and in that state of mind. They'd be in the emergency room right now, arguing in intense whispers, rather than him in a ward with a banged up head and broken leg and Brenton…wherever Brenton was. Jake didn't even know whether he was okay.

He knew Brenton well enough to know that the entire situation had escalated out of control. Brenton would have stupidly poisoned Christie, without any concept of reality, justifying it fully to himself, telling himself he could have told the hospital about what had happened at any time. Instead, he'd slid into an obsessed spiral, desperate to love and be loved, to be with the man of his dreams. He might have paid the ultimate price.

He winced as he peered around the room. There appeared to be three other beds. The one directly across from him contained an obese, snoring old man, while the occupant of the bed directly to his right could not be seen because of the curtains pulled around it. No sound emanated from that direction though, so maybe the curtains weren't being used for privacy reasons. The bed diagonally opposite had been stripped bare.

Jake groaned as he fished for some type of nurse notification button. After fumbling around above his head, clattering and patting various items surrounding the bed, he eventually found a gray cylinder with a red button wedged between the mattress and the bed frame. He pressed it and a muted buzz registered in the corridor. Jake cocked an ear, hoping for approaching footsteps. He closed his eyes in an attempt to relax, but the picture remained in his mind. A tall girl appeared to the right of the windscreen, her blonde hair swaying as she scurried after the cocker spaniel pup. Her left leg was inches away from the grille. In slow motion, Brenton had swung the steering wheel to the left where it clicked as it locked.

He'd come to with his head embedded in the visor. A river of blood ran down Brenton's forehead, which had lodged in the windscreen, glass embedded into the skin. A paramedic with watery eyes had spoken to him, but his words were indecipherable. After moving his hands and fingers, he and his partner had moved Jake delicately onto the stretcher. Then he'd let the blackness overtake him.

A rustle to the left caught his attention and he opened his eyes. A dark-skinned nurse with short hair fussed with the sheet.

"Can I help you?"

"My friend Brenton, where is he? The driver of the car when we crashed?"

She regarded him blankly. "He's in another ward." Her lips pressed together in a frown, and she recommenced sheet rearrangements.

"Which ward? Can I see him?"

"Not now. He's in ICU." She wouldn't look at him.

"Intensive care? Is he okay? What happened to him?

"He sustained a brain injury."

"Brain injury? As in what? Will he be the same person?" He strained his neck in an unsuccessful attempt to sit up.

The nurse continued to fuss with the bed sheets, but eventually she met his gaze. It told him all he needed to know.

Jake couldn't speak. He touched his temple and closed his eyes, wishing that he and Brenton could jump back in time. If only he'd done things differently, taken control, shaken some sense into him. The nurse's soft footsteps echoed as she retreated. An uncontrollable whimper escaped as he imagined Brenton in intensive care, a mass of tangled tubes, unconscious and unfeeling.

Burning tears gathered, and he wondered if Brenton would be a vegetable or if he'd recover in time. Such a damned mess. He sobbed until pain surged through his chest.

Brenton was screwed up and twisted, of that, he was certain, yet in that moment, Jake ached for his friend. Underneath the insecurities, the obsessions lurked a good man, neurotic and desperately lonely.

Jake sucked in a breath and attempted to slow down his breathing and gain control. He'd find out from the doctor later about his friend's condition. He hoped to hell that he'd imagined the worst conclusion; he'd love to be completely wrong. Maybe that way Brenton would recover.

***

EPILOGUE

Wednesday 23rd January, 9.07am

Christie sat upright in bed, her skin warm and the beginning of a smile making its way across her face.

She reached for the cup of tea on the trolley table to her right, and brought it to her lips when Ryan rushed in. His face lit up as he saw her. He bounded to her bedside, and she set the cup down just as he enveloped her in a warm hug. Over Ryan's shoulder, Christie saw Connor peer around the doorway before he entered the room. A grin and a tight grip of her hand were the only indications of his relief.

Ryan pulled away and with wobbly legs lowered himself onto the chair beside her bed.

"Thank god you're okay," he said.

Connor let go of her hand and sat on the edge of the bed. "We're so glad you recovered. We were so worried about you," he said, flicking a glance at Ryan.

"I heard the nurses talking. Gypsy was right, wasn't she? I was poisoned and too stubborn to listen." Christie's chin dropped. "I'm so sorry—"

Connor brought a palm up before resting it on her arm. He swung his knees around toward her. "That's nothing to worry about. Gypsy will be as happy as we are that you're okay. Your safety is all she's thought about for days."

Christie picked up her cup to take a sip and placed it back down.

Ryan smiled at her. "You don't know how good it is to see you do that." Such a simple gesture, one that he had wondered if he'd ever see again. Relief surged through him and he sat forward in the chair with elbows on his knees shaking his head. Connor stood up quickly as Gypsy appeared in the doorway. She bounded in to stand at the bottom of the bed. Her face flushed and her eyes brightened as they met Christies.'

"Oh my god you're okay! What a bloody relief!" she said with a shaky laugh.

Christie extended her arms to Gypsy. "Come here, you."

Gypsy moved forward. Christie gripped her in an embrace, rubbing her back. Gypsy turned to face Connor, and he gave her a thumbs-up.

Gypsy pulled away and Christie spoke. "I heard the staff talking. Apparently they received an anonymous note about what happened." She flushed. "The poisoning, I mean. You saved me, didn't you? Even after the shitty way I treated you."

Gypsy breathed deeply. "I know we haven't always seen eye to eye, but I had to stop this, I couldn't have it on my conscience. I know how much you mean to Connor." Ryan met her gaze. "To all of us."

Christie's shoulders curved. "I have a confession." She licked her lips and swallowed hard. "I've been visiting Aaron for a while now." Her chin quivered. "It was stupid, I know that now. Of course he tried to kill you so I knew he'd be biased." A smile made its way across her face and her eyes glinted. "Not that you're entirely blameless Gypsy, but it's time to move on. I guess I just wanted family near me, some reassurance. He fed me the venom that was meant for you. Can we start over? We've got a way to go before we're best friends but…"

"Of course we can." Gypsy's face brightened even further. "Your hallucinations about torturing evil Gypsy-bitches kind of gave you away." Gypsy managed a smile, and Christie, Connor and Ryan burst out laughing.

"Can we give things another try?" asked Christie.

"Of course we can," Gypsy said then patted Christie's knee.

⁂

Wednesday 23rd January, 9.12am

I'd wondered about Christie's recovery, but the sight of her pink cheeks told me all I needed to know. We'd come full circle. After clearing the air, I'd never been closer to Connor. Life didn't get much better.

After heartfelt apologies and all-round clearing of the air, the conversation took a turn upward.

I saw a shadow behind me and turned to see what could only be a doctor dressed in white shirt, navy dress pants and ruffled hair. He stood several feet away from us, hesitating to join the conversation.

"Sorry to interrupt. I'm Dr. Blackmore. I thought your family might like an update." He came to stand beside Ryan, who rose from his chair and took Christie's hand.

"Yes," Ryan said, color rising back into his face. He stood up and his eyes brightened.

Dr. Blackmore cleared his throat. "Well, I'm pleased to see you're feeling better."

Christie nodded. "I'm so relieved. I'm not really sure how long I was unconscious for, but I overheard the nurses talking…" Her smile faded, and she fiddled with the fingers on her right hand.

The doctor glanced at Ryan before transferring his eyes back to Christie.

"You were affected by antifreeze, that much we do know." The doctor paused, blinking rapidly. "Have you considered pressing charges?"

Ryan's nostrils flared and he raised his eyebrows revealing the whites of his eyes.

"We have," he said, speaking through gritted teeth.

"We need to talk," said Connor.

The doctor took events in before moving to Christie's side. A frown marred her previously smooth forehead. Her mouth opened and closed a couple of times before she managed to speak.

"We do?" she said.

"Yeah. We know who the poisoner is." At that moment, the smell of bleach overpowered me.

The doctor took a step back. "I'll give you some private time."

"No, don't! Stay, please." Christie closed her eyes and fell back against the pillow, shoulders hunched. Connor sighed and retrieved his mobile telephone from a back pocket. "I got a message on the way here. Brenton and Jake are in the same hospital. He's in intensive care, but Jake should recover. Brenton is another story…"

"Brenton?" In an instant, Christie jerked up as if her spine had been transformed into a rod of iron. "Not Brenton…" she dissolved into a mess of tears.

Ryan pressed a hand to the bed head for support and cleared his throat.

Connor sat on the bed beside her and patted her leg "I'm so, so sorry Christie. This never should have happened."

Her eyes filled and her chin wobbled. "But, he's my best friend, he wouldn't–"

Up until this point, I'd stayed in the background, an observer watching events unfold rather than taking an active role. My psychic detective work, of course, couldn't be mentioned or we'd become laughingstocks. I knew somehow that the slightest word would be the straw that could destroy the entire facade. I'd been there before in my younger years and I damn well didn't want to go there again. I'd just have to ride this one out.

I took a step closer to Connor.

"Why would Brenton do that to me?" Christie sobbed. "We were friends."

"Put simply, I believe it was jealousy," Connor told her. Christie didn't seem capable of speech, so he continued. "He wanted Ryan."

Christie sobbed harder. I detected "Oh my god" amongst her cries.

The doctor seemed unsure whether to stay or leave. He stood to Connor's left.

A breeze blew across my face, but possibly, only I perceived it.

From the corner of my eye, I saw her. She stood between Ryan and Christie, one hand holding his, the other stroking Christie's hair.

Isabella.

For the first time ever, she smiled. Not a grin, but a full-blown, beaming smile.

Weird.

"You shouldn't stress yourself," the doctor said. "Not in your condition,"

All four of our heads snapped toward him. Isabella continued to beam.

The doctor cleared his throat. "When we checked your blood, and tested your urine for crystals of ethylene glycol, we discovered that you're pregnant. We'll monitor the pregnancy, of course, but with the antidote administered in time, everything should be okay."

In the tears and overjoyed hugging that followed, I barely noticed my spirit child friend preparing to leave. When I lifted my head and wiped the dampness from under my eyes, I saw Isabella wave a goodbye as she drifted away.

I almost missed her. It wouldn't be *goodbye,* though, simply *see you later*. We'd have plenty of time to catch up after she was born. I looked forward to getting to know more about her.

Isabella had saved Christie's life and had brought us together as no one else could. Maybe she always intended to do so.

I'd never forget her and her cryptic ways. Sounded like someone else I knew.

Connor kissed his niece and murmured, "Congratulations honey."

"Congratulations. You're going to be a grandfather."

Connor's mouth flew open and he gasped, posture stiffening.

"You–you knew all this time?"

Christie flushed, her smile spreading. "It wasn't hard to figure out. Neither was the fact that you obviously didn't want to talk about it."

Ryan looked at them both. "You're her father?"

"Seems that way," I said, speaking for Connor who, for the moment, struggled to speak further. "He must have asked for a paternity test at the same time as the blood test. Good news all round." I rubbed Connor's back and kissed him on the cheek.

"We'll give you two a bit of time alone," I said before taking Connor's hand, and guiding him away from the happy couple.

Ryan tipped his head up and blew out a breath, dropping his chin to beam at his girlfriend.

Connor took my hand and followed me out to the corridor. I draped my arm around his waist, and he returned the embrace.

"I can't believe it!" he said, his smile widening, eyes bright.

"Believe it," I said, moving closer. He grabbed me then, his hands in the small of my back, burning through my light clothing.

His lips were soft and urgent, demanding nothing but giving his all.

"Congratulations, you old fart," I said when the kiss broke, happiness surging in my chest.

"Come on," Connor said, linking my arm through his. "Let's celebrate."

So we did.

***

-THE END-

About the Author

Andrea Drew has been a commercial copywriter and resume writer for over a decade.

She's written for celebrity stylists, assisted business coaches and start-ups, written grants for not for profits, delivered marketing presentations to business owners, and attended Australian writing conventions.

Andrea has one husband (more than enough), three kids, a pet rock (her daughter's not hers), and a house in the suburbs, where she's hard at work on the final book in the Gypsy Series and the first in her second fiction series to be released in early 2016.

The Gypsy Series can be read as standalones or in the following recommended order:

In 2015

The Gypsy Series
Gypsy Life - Prequel/Story
Book #1 - Gypsy Hunted
Book #2 - Gypsy Cradle
Book #3 - Gypsy Curse

In 2016
The Sentinel Series
Return of the Sentinel
Saved by the Sentinel
Son of the Sentinel

Short Story Collection
Twisted Tales

Non-Fiction
Pro Resumes Made Easy
Government Job Apps Made Easy

She can be contacted via her blog:
www.andreadrewauthor.com

or via GoodReads here:
https://www.goodreads.com/andreadrew

Gypsy Life – An Excerpt

As a child, growing up in the outer eastern suburbs of Melbourne, I never thought of ghosts as strange, weird or shameful in any way shape or form (pardon the pun). As an adult later in life, of course I leaned much more toward the skeptical side of ghostly apparitions and things that go bump in the night, but as events unfolded, I had no choice. I had to accept I could do things other people seemingly couldn't. My parents managed to knock out any predilection I had towards the spiritual and/or ghostly world well and truly—probably due to their own inbuilt terror of all matters nonphysical. If it couldn't be seen, touched or observed by the majority of the population then quite simply it didn't exist.

It probably didn't help that I unwittingly talked to the previous property owner, who to all intents and purposes was actually deceased. As a small child, I had absolutely no thought or consideration that this woman was dead, although I did think at the time that she was just a tad bit forceful and not best pleased with my mother.

Padding softly along the upstairs landing and into mum and dad's room due to yet another nocturnal visitor, I remember vividly lying in between them as most young children are wont to do and having trouble sleeping due to this woman/apparition moving restlessly around the bottom of Mum and Dad's bed, gesturing wildly.

If anything, she was supremely annoying if not persistent and just would not leave things well alone. She doggedly shoved messages, thoughts and pictures into what was the majority of the time a blank canvas of a mind, from her point of view anyway, I'm sure.

—Oh for goodness sakes, I said to her mentally. *I'll tell her in the morning.*

Nevertheless, no this old dear wasn't taking no for an answer.

—Wake her up, wake her up or she'll forget.

—No I won't, she's asleep! I'm not waking her up just so you can talk to her. They already think I'm a bit touched in the head, even though kids aren't supposed to be aware of adults talking about us as if we're not in the room.

—Yes children should be seen and not heard.

—Of course you would say that. So why don't you talk to her yourself then?

—You are an extremely rude and insolent young girl. If you don't tell her, I will and I don't think you'll be too pleased with the manner in which I inform her.

—All right. I said to this old dear wearily, not knowing or caring what her name was. I did however realize at this point that obviously this old biddy was aware that it would be much easier for her to talk to me than it was to talk to mum and dad

which would require an almost herculean effort on her part.

So she wasn't going away in a hurry.

Talking to people who no longer technically have a body is, to put it mildly, very draining as a grown up. As a child, however, I had no concept of this. My parents certainly provided me with a few concepts.

"Stop, don't do that, she won't like it. No!" I said out loud sitting up bolt upright in the bed. "No, it's not. It's my mum's, not yours. No, don't try to pick that up. It's hers now, not yours. You're confused." The old dear was venturing towards Mum's dressing table, criticizing the items she had on there, in particular an antique hairbrush which she claimed was 'crass' and 'mutton dressed as lamb.'

I'm sure that mum had woken up prior to this but had conveniently chosen to ignore my rantings as that of an imaginative and sleep-disturbed child. My parents would later tell me I was "a bit nervy" like my maternal grandmother, the Romani Gypsy, Dee. I now prefer to use the term "fae."

Fae according to Wikipedia (the Mother of all things authoritative or not so authoritative depending upon your viewpoint and the amount of spare time on one's hands) is defined as:

a. Having or displaying an otherworldly, magical, or fairylike aspect or quality: "She's got that fae look as though she's had breakfast with a leprechaun" (Dorothy Burnham).

b. Having visionary power; clairvoyant.

C. appearing touched or crazy, as if under a spell.

Although of course I'm not sure how I feel about being fated to die soon?

a. Fated to die soon.

b. Full of the sense of approaching death.

Although of course, I *love* the romantic notion of being a fairy or elf and a person of magical properties.

[Middle English feie, fated to die, from Old English fge.]

In a very un-fae like way, my mother's voice at this point took on a noticeable tone of terror or as terrified as you can be around 3am in the still quiet of morning in a darkened room with a young daughter talking to thin air.

"Ernie! *Ern*! Shut her up, will you. She's awake." she was trying to whisper but the hoarseness in her too-quiet voice was giving her away.

Dad rolled over halfway.

"Uh? Wha? What are you going on about?"

"Gypsy. Talk to her, will you. She's woken up. I think she's dreaming."

"I'm *not* dreaming! I'm talking to that woman over *there*. Can't you see her? She's right there. *Right there*! Look dad there she is!"

At this point dad sighed, probably filled with the impatience of yet another night's broken sleep from an "imaginative" child and a wife that called his name whenever something needed to be 'sorted out' that she didn't want to bother with, me being too hard to deal with and all that.

"Gypsy," he said his voice still thick with sleep. "What's all this then? Come on now, back to sleep eh? It's late and we all have to get up in the morning." His voice had taken on a kindly, 'us against them' tone but I could sense the condescension creeping in.

"Da-a-ad! She's right there, look! She doesn't like Mum being in her room! She says it's her room and the furniture's rearranged the wrong way and she keeps trying to pick up mum's things on the dressing table. She says this is her house and doesn't want us here."

At this point Dad sat up. I almost felt sorry for him, or would if I had understood at this point, what he would go through later in life.

"Eh? What do you mean she doesn't want us here?"

At this point, my strong silent Father was beginning to sound a *teeny* bit alarmed.

"This is her house dad. She wants to know what we're doing in it. She says that mum's dressing table shouldn't be there, that's where her chair goes. And she says we would be better off finding somewhere else to live."

Dad got up and got dressed, obviously resigning himself to the fact that there was no more sleep to be had this night. He picked me up and carried me back to bed in the top bunk. My sister as usual was obliviously unconscious in the bunk below.

We had a nice long chat about how dead people 'aren't really there, we just think they are.'

This was enough to introvert me for a good twenty minutes before I finally nodded off.

Of course, the next morning I forgot all about it. At the breakfast table, Mum obliquely referred to it as she was dishing out breakfast onto a plate I barely registered existed, and I shrugged her comments off with an 'I don't know neither do I care' type gesture.

I vividly recall being up late at night and sneaking halfway down the stairs a few nights later as I was so wickedly prone to do, only to hear dad talking to mum about how he was sure the last person to live there was an old woman and maybe they could find out more about it?

Little did they know.

***

www.ingramcontent.com/pod-product-compliance
Lightning Source LLC
Chambersburg PA
CBHW020420110726
47899CB00006B/2066